Tales of a Kitchen Witch

Also, by Adrienne Lee

My Magical Awakening: A Journey in Real Black Girl Magic

The 369 Manifestation Journal

Tales of a Kitchen Witch

By Adrienne Lee

ISBN: 9798844488825

Dedication

This book is dedicated to my son, Demarco Lee Lopes.

One day when you're old enough you will read this book and be proud of your Mommy.

PROLOGUE

Never in a million years would I have thought that I would be a full fledge practicing witch. In my inner circle, my nick name is the "Kitchen Witch" because everything I need can be found in my kitchen. From sage, to sugar, and even honey, I use what is in my kitchen to strengthen my spells. When I first began my journey most of my family condemned me and my path to become a witch, but they have learned to accept me and my witchy ways especially when they need me to cast a spell on their behalf. Not only has my family embraced my abilities but I have fully stepped into my power and no longer hide from the spotlight. I also decided to learn everything about witchcraft by receiving mentorship and guidance from Miss Jay, who is a spiritual teacher of witchcraft and metaphysics. I am glad to say that I am on my way to completing the mentorship which has helped me to use my physical and mental abilities like I never have before. While I am still perfecting my craft, I have been able to master the use of herbs which is another reason why I love being a Kitchen Witch. While I embrace being a witch, using that term to describe myself still sounds kind of funny to me. I can barely believe it, just two years ago I hated when others would call me a witch because I hadn't fully embraced my calling. It's funny how things can change, because now I am a proud spell casting Kitchen Witch. Yep, I said it, Witch! Many people get turned off when they hear that word because they are afraid that I may put a spell on them but have no fear, I only use my magic for good. That is, unless you have wronged me but let's not go down that road. The road I am going to take you on today, is my path to freedom and empowerment. Come along with me and share my experiences of being a Kitchen Witch.

CHAPTER 1
THE LAST RITES

I can't believe it; I had made it to my last rite. Leaving my house for the ceremony, I felt excited but nervous. I was dressed in all white as Miss Jay had instructed us to do. While I was used to the stereotype that all witches wore black, we were instructed to wear white since it signifies purity of the mind, body, and soul. Not only does white signify purity but it also helps to cleanse away old energy and bring in new beginnings. Tonight, was going to be the start of a new beginning in my magical journey. Throughout this journey I have had to go through different rites to get to this point. The rites consisted of completing several assignments and mastering skills that were essential to being a witch practicing magic.

However, before any rites could take place, we had to learn protection. Protection is the first thing that Miss Jay taught us. She would always say, "No spells without protection." This was a must when casting spells because you never knew who or what was out to get you and could potentially cause your spell to backfire. To prove that I knew how to protect myself, I created a protection charm to ward off negativity. The protection charm I created was a black tourmaline crystal bracelet that I wear everywhere I go. This bracelet has been programmed to protect me along with magnifying black tourmaline's natural protective energy.

After learning protection, the first rite was to ask for the ancestors' permission to access the spirit world. During this rite which lasted for weeks, I had to write down every name that I knew from previous generations that had passed on and give them offerings. Offerings consisted of water, wine, and even tobacco but that was the easy part. The last piece was to give them an offering of my blood. Even though, I was ready for this journey I was not prepared to give up my blood. I had seen this type of thing in the movies and at first it seemed like a pact you make with the devil, but Miss Jay squashed those nervous feelings that I had. She said, "Do not be afraid because blood is what connects you to your ancestors and they made sacrifices for you. Giving a drop of your blood is easy compared to what they went through for you to be here." Her words made me change my mind about being scared and if a drop of blood can repay my ancestors for what they've done for me, I was all in. At that point all I could do was go ahead and prick my finger. I squeamishly watched the blood drip onto the paper as she then burned it. After that rite, I felt a closeness to my ancestors as I never had before. My ancestors have been a vital piece in my journey in every way possible. When I ask them for insight and guidance they always come through. That feeling I get when I am going left and something says go right, that's them. I can hardly believe that was my first rite and now I was going to be facing the last rite in my journey.

As I pulled up to Miss Jay's shop, I sat in the car before going in with the hopes of calming my nerves. Times like this I wish I smoked so I could relax myself. Since I am not a smoker, I sat in my car and took a deep breath. I sat and watched my other fellow witches enter the building. There were two other witches along side of me in the mentorship. While I had never been in a sorority, I felt like these ladies went through the fire with me, those burning sands as they would say. Just like a sorority we had nick names. I was the "Kitchen Witch". I took on that name proudly due to the fact that I loved working with herbs. When I was younger, I remember my Aunt Nadine having a cabinet full of herbs, spices, and oils and they weren't just for cooking. She would pull out her herbs and roots to make all types of potions and spells. I guess I inherited those skills because I now had jars and bottles filled with all kinds of herbs such as lavender, lemon grass, and even flowers like rose petals. At some point I became obsessed with herbs. Every day I would find myself researching herbs and their magical properties. Now I am to the point that I know the smells and looks of just about every herb that there is. While I mastered herbs, my fellow witches went about their magic in a different way.

Jewel, who we nicknamed the "Christian Witch," was not at all into herbs like me. Being nicknamed the Christian Witch she was a Bible toting, Bible verse reciting type of witch. I was surprised when I found out that she attended church just about every Sunday and even sang on the choir. Everyone in the church knew what she did and to be honest they would ask for her help when their prayers did not work. She would always say, "God gave me the gift to cast spells so there is nothing wrong with what I do, and I dare anyone else to tell me otherwise." With that strong conviction no one could tell her she was wrong even the most conservative Christians gave her respect and sought her out for help. I was so impressed with the way she balanced her faith in God as well as her beliefs with magic.

Then there was Drea, she was called the "Spirit Witch." She got that name because she could call upon spirits of the dead, including heavenly beings such as angels. She was able to channel angels and communicate with them to guide others on their right path. Her connection with the angels and ancestors allowed her to give great advice because of the guidance she received from the other side. I was so impressed with her talents and abilities because I knew I was too scared to channel spirits. While we each had our own unique abilities, we always respected and helped each other when one of us were in need. When it was all said and done, I knew these ladies had my back, front, and side. We were bonded for life.

After finally calming my nerves, I took one last breath and I walked into the building and greeted my fellow sisters. We all made our way into the dark room and took our seats. Our Mentor, Miss Jay stood quietly watching us one by one. As she took her place in front of us, she instructed us to rise and stand in our power. We all stood as instructed and as I stood my heart was beating so fast as if it was going to jump out of my chest. I didn't know what to expect that night as I was receiving my last rite in my magical journey.

With all of us standing, Miss Jay asked each of us one by one were we ready to receive our last rite. When it was my turn, I said, "Yes," with my voice shaking.

She said, “Now Kitchen Witch you seem like you’re scared, I didn’t raise no scared witches.”

I sighed, and with a slight smile I remembered to stand in my power and said, “You’re right, I AM READY!”

“That’s more like it,” Miss Jay said.

After that we all stood and held hands. We all promised to have each other’s back and to always remember the strong witches that we are.

Miss Jay then said, “I want each of you to take this pin to prick your finger and drop your blood into the candle. This blood rite is the last one in your journey with me. It signifies the power you will inherit, and it bonds you not only with your ancestral bloodline but with the women who stand before you. Each of your bloodlines will benefit from what you are doing today. Not only are you bonded by the blood, but this signifies the sacrifice that you made to get here. You will now claim your power from the ancestors and solidify your connection to each other. Now repeat after me.”

When she started to speak it sounded as if she was speaking Latin or even Hebrew. ‘Til this day I don’t know the language she spoke but because of the trust I had in her, without hesitation I recited the words in unison with the other girls while watching the flame on the candle flicker.

After we were done Ms. Jay said, “You have completed my teachings and your rites. I know you don’t feel it now but soon after you will feel different and see changes in your life. From this point on, your life is forever changed, and it will be for the better. Not a day goes by that I don’t use magic and call upon my ancestors and you will start to do the same.”

As she looked at each one of us smiling, she said, “I thank you girls for trusting me and allowing me to teach you all, and I thank the ancestors, the Universe, and the Almighty Creator. Now, I urge each of you girls to give thanks to those who assisted you in this journey.”

I was the first to stand up and give thanks but as I stood, I was at a loss for words. While holding my candle I began to cry as this intense emotion came over me. Then something deep inside of me gave me the strength to stop crying. Once I gathered my thoughts, I thanked the ancestors and the spirits who guide me from the other side of the veil. I thanked my sisters and Miss Jay for their support and guidance. Then I yelled, "I am thankful for all my newfound knowledge, and I will use it in any capacity that I see fit because I am the master of my life."

Then Miss Jay chimed in and said, "Ayanna, it's okay to be emotional, this is you letting go of the old you and embracing the new. I know you like to keep your emotions inside but it's good to let them out. I am proud that you were able to let your guard down and share your feelings with us. Now who's up next?"

Jewel said, "I am." Jewel stood up and spoke of her love for God and how he showed her the path to magic. I smiled, because I was glad to see her merge her love for God and magic together. The next words out of her mouth were, "Not only do I serve a great God who has brought me to magic, but I am a Goddess myself! I thank each one of you for believing in my greatness and being there when I was conflicted with myself and my beliefs." As she finished, we all clapped, and then Drea, the bold "Spirit Witch" stood. She shouted and said, "I first want to thank the entire team of Spirits who guide me!"

As Drea finished her speech, Miss Jay smiled and said, "Not too many make it, but I am glad you three were the ones to do it. I call y'all the Power of Three...The Three Horsemen or better yet the Trinity. Three is the perfect number, it means harmony and optimism and that's what I see for you all in the future. You all complement each other so well and are powerful in your own right but together you all can make things happen, trust me. Furthermore, you all are the Goddesses that I knew you could become. I am proud of each one of you as you take your last rite."

We then sat our candles down, held hands, and spoke the words, "I am my ancestors, and we are one. The power of three we will forever be." As we finished Miss Jay said, "This is your last rite and you have made it."

We all looked at each other, smiled and sighed with relief knowing we made it through the fire. It was a long six months but worth it. Then Miss Jay turned on the lights and said, "Okay girls the serious stuff is over, now we can party and celebrate!"

We opened some champagne and put on some music. We danced and had so much fun that night. On the way home I felt electrified and happy because I knew my Aunt Nadine would've been so proud of me for taking this bold step. I couldn't wait for my new life to start. While studying was intense, I hardly did any spells since I was learning but now was the time to take all that I learned and use it in my everyday life.

As I drove home, I thought about my life and how the last year felt like a dream. Being someone who was taught to be afraid of spells and magic, I never thought that I would be a magical Goddess in my own right. I felt so empowered like I could do anything and have everything I wanted out of life.

As I made it home, my husband, Rashad, eagerly wanted to know what went on. As soon as I walked into the door he asked, "So how did it go?"

I said, "I was nervous in the beginning, but it turned out to be great. We went through our last rites and then we partied for the rest of the night. I feel so powerful right now, like I can conjure up a million dollars."

He then replied, "Damn, well how about you go conjure up some money for me. Better yet let's go to the bedroom so you can conjure up some of your good loving."

I said, "You know what, that's not a bad idea. You know there is a thing called sex magic."

He said, "Really? Well, I want all the magic you got. Come and show me some of that black girl magic you always talking about."

I laughed and said, “You’re crazy but come on let's go to bed. I will show you everything I learned about sex magic.”

CHAPTER 2
THE NEIGHBORS FROM HELL

When I woke up the next morning, I was excited but sad that I would no longer see Miss Jay and the girls on a regular basis. Miss Jay was always encouraging, and the girls gave me a sense of comfort because I was able to talk to them about magic. Who else could I talk to about crystals and seeing spirits? I sat on the edge of my bed thinking about how much my life has changed. I decided to pick up my journal and write down my thoughts but as I began to write I heard loud music blasting. As I walked outside, I noticed that the music was coming from Kimmey and Joe, my neighbors' from across the street, AKA the neighbors from hell. My life has been a living hell since they moved into our neighborhood.

They play their music loud as hell at night and then have the nerve to come over almost every other day to beg for a ride to the store or to borrow every household item you can name. It got so bad one day they wanted to borrow toilet paper, I mean who borrows toilet paper? When I told them I didn't have any toilet paper to share, they asked me to take them to the store instead. Since I wasn't going to take them to the store, I gave in and let them have a roll of toilet paper. To be honest I didn't want to take them to the store because knowing them they probably would have stolen it or sold their food stamps for money, and you can bet I was not going to be caught up with that drama.

I tried to ignore their loud music, but it was just irritating me even more as I stood there. I walked into the living room to tell my husband about it because this madness had to stop.

I asked him, "Rashad, don't you hear that loud music coming from across the street?"

He said, "Yes, but that's just Kimmey. You know she's just loud and ghetto."

I said, "Well, I don't care, it's bothering me. You need to let them know that they are being too loud. If I go over there, I may curse them out."

Rashad then said, "Oh, so it's my responsibility?"

I say, "Well yea, you are the man in this relationship, right? Plus, they think you're their friend. You're always speaking to them and carrying on conversations, so yea."

Reluctantly, Rashad said, "Okay, I will go over in a second."

I went back to my room and waited for my husband come back. He seemed to be gone for about an hour, but the music had stopped so I guess he was able to talk some sense into them.

Finally, I heard Rashad come into the house. I yelled out and asked him, "Rashad, where have you been?"

He walked into the room and said, "I know I was gone a long time but I ended up taking Joe and Kimmey to the store so they could buy some cigarettes and stuff."

I say, "Rashad, are you serious?"

He says, "Yea what's the problem? That got them to turn the music down, didn't it?"

As I look at him and roll my eyes, the doorbell rings. It was the neighbor, Joe.

As soon as I opened the door, Joe said, "Hey y'all. I got my cigarettes, but I don't have a lighter." He then begged, "Can I borrow a lighter please?"

I say, "Okay", then I give him a lighter so he could light his cigarette. As I wait for him to give it back, he says, "Oh, can I take this home for a minute so my Old Lady can light her cigarette?"

I look at him and say, "Really", then just to get him out of my face, I say, "Okay go ahead."

Soon as Joe leaves, I tell Rashad, "See, what did I tell you, they're always mooching off people, and you can bet I will never see that lighter again."

Surprisingly Rashad agreed with me and said, "Yea they are annoying but what else can we do?"

Based on his response, it was obvious that Rashad had no plans on confronting the neighbors about their behavior. So, just like a teenage girl, I sucked my teeth and rolled my eyes as I went to my bedroom to find some peace and quiet.

As the day went on, I tried to relax and do some meditating. As I began to meditate my son, Amir comes in the room. He asked me if he could go across the street to play with the neighbors' kids. First, I tell him no, but he begs me so I give in and tell him he can go play.

I watched Amir as he walked across the street and as I stood there, I decided that this would be a good time to meditate. I loved being in nature and the grass felt so good on my feet. As I sat down in the grass and started to meditate, I couldn't help but to notice my neighbors watching me. I knew they probably thought I was crazy out here in the grass but what the hell, they're crazy in my eyes.

As I meditated, I was startled by screams coming from across the street. I immediately looked over at the neighbors' yard and saw my son and the neighbor's child screaming while dogs chased them. They made their way into my yard, and I closed the gate so the dogs couldn't get in. The dogs continued to bark and tried to jump over the fence. I yelled and told my son and his friend to get into the house and I followed behind them and closed the door.

As I ran into the house, I screamed for my husband, "Rashad, Rashad, where are you!"

Rashad walked in the room and calmly responded, "What is it? Why are you screaming like that, Ayanna?"

After a deep sigh, I say, "What is it? I will tell you what it is, those people gotta go! Amir got chased by their dogs. Didn't you hear him screaming and running in the house?"

Rashad then says, "Oh, I wasn't paying attention and I had the door closed."

I tell him, "Well, I was there watching, and those dogs are dangerous. You have got to do something about them!"

Rashad says, "I know you and Amir were scared of those dogs but Baby we can't kick them out we are not the police."

Annoyed by Rashad's response, I say, "We may not be the police, but we sure can call the police about those dogs."

I couldn't believe Rashad was being all laid back about the dogs chasing us. He needed to step up and be a man and protect his family. I just stood there waiting for him to do something.

Then finally he said, "Yea you're right about that, but I am going to talk to the neighbors first. I know you don't think I am doing enough but I want to talk to Joe man to man to see what can be done first before calling the police."

After assuring me that he would take care of it, Rashad went outside and spoke with the neighbors. As he came back home, I eagerly awaited to see what they discussed.

Soon as he came through the door, I asked, "So, what did he say?"

Rashad said, "Joe said he is going to have the dogs put down or let them live with his brother because of what happened. He said the dogs are usually tied up but somehow, they got loose."

I say, "Okay. Well, I am glad you talked to him but like I said I don't want Amir in harm's way especially if he goes over there to play with their kids. You need to make sure that they get rid of those dogs, you hear me, Rashad?"

Rashad then says, “Yea I hear you but why don’t you do something about it, Ayanna? You’re the big bad witch, why don’t you do a spell or something to make them stop.”

I couldn’t believe Rashad said that to me. I was somewhat offended because I didn’t know if he was throwing shade, or if he really wanted me to do something because he was too lazy to do it himself. Whatever the case was, I stood there for a minute trying to understand the motives behind his words.

Then I confidently said, “You know what, you ain’t got to say another word, Rashad. You can believe I’m on it.”

After our conversation, I was determined to find the best spell to get rid of unwanted neighbors. All this time putting up with their mess, I should have been doing magic on their ghetto asses.

I take out my journal and begin getting the pieces together for my spell.

Being a true, “Kitchen Witch,” I found all I needed in my kitchen. Black pepper, vinegar, and some cayenne pepper. I was going to create a banishment jar for my neighbors so they could get the hell on. Later that night I took out my materials, added all the items to the jar and shook it up. I then took a piece of paper and wrote down my neighbor’s names and simply wrote, “MOVE OUT” on the paper. I sat the jar on top of the paper and lit a candle. As the candle burned, I spoke a simple rhyme for my spell, “Neighbors be gone, I command you to find a new home.”

As the candle burned, I couldn’t help but to think how good my life would be after they move out. The best part about casting spells was anticipating the outcome and I knew they would be gone in no time with the help of my spell.

Later that night, as I made my way into bed, Rashad had the nerve to ask me, “Ayanna, what have you been doing downstairs all this time?”

"What do you think I have been doing? You told me to get a spell to make the neighbors move out, so that's what I have been doing."

"Oh, I didn't know you were going to do that for real."

"Rashad, you know how I do. I don't talk about it; I be about it. And if the spell works like it should, they should be gone in no time."

"Really, how do you know that?"

"I just do, now don't be questioning me and my skills."

The next morning while getting Amir on the school bus, I couldn't help but to look over at the neighbor's yard. I kept thinking about going over there to confront them about their dogs, but I have faith in my spell. I am just going to wait and see what happens.

As I walked back into the house, Rashad tells me, "Good morning."

I simply reply, "Good morning. How are you?"

"I'm good but I don't think you are. I see you over there eyeing the neighbor's house," said Rashad.

I tell him, "Yes, I was. I really wanted to go over there and curse them out for letting those dogs chase Amir. I am still pissed off about that, but my spell will give them what they deserve. Furthermore, I don't think they have any plans of getting rid of those dogs. They probably only told you that to stop you from calling the police."

"Yea you're probably right but when I get home from work, I will go over there and see if Joe really plans on getting rid of those dogs," Rashad said.

I was glad that Rashad was finally taking initiative to get the dogs gone. I told him, "Thank you that would be great." I then gave him a kiss on the cheek and said, "I am going to get dressed. I will see you later."

Once Rashad returned home from work, I peeped out the window and saw him talking to Joe. Joe stood there talking with a cigarette hanging halfway out of his mouth. That man was always running his mouth about something. More than likely talking about his "Old Lady" as he would say. I can only imagine what he's telling Rashad.

When Rashad came in, I could tell Joe had told him something. I eagerly asked, "What was Joe talking about out there?"

Rashad then said, "Let's just say I think your spell worked."

I looked at him with a puzzled look on my face and said, "Huh, what happened?"

Sitting down at the kitchen table, Rashad starts to tell me the story. He says, "Well Joe told me their landlord came by their house today. Apparently, someone in the neighborhood contacted the landlord about the dogs. I guess they saw the dogs chasing Amir and his friend. The landlord told Joe that he could not have dogs on the property which was forbidden in his lease. So, the landlord decided to evict him. Joe said they will have to move out by the end of the month."

You should have seen the look on my face when Rashad told me this. My mouth was wide open, and I was shocked as hell that my spell worked so fast. And to think I didn't even have to call the police or the landlord but that's how magic works. I just put the ball in motion and let the universe do the rest.

After getting over the initial shock, I say, "Dang, that's crazy but that's what they get."

Agreeing with me, Rashad says, "Yea, those dogs were dangerous but now Joe is complaining because they don't know where they are going to live now."

I say, "You know what Rashad, I hate to say it but they got what they deserve."

He says, "I know, but I guess I feel bad for them."

I look at Rashad, roll my eyes and say, "I don't feel a bit sorry for them. I certainly will not miss their loud music, late night fighting and all those damn dogs. It's about time they get out."

After a couple days had passed, I was surprised that the neighbors were staying to themselves. Usually, I see them outside or hear them blasting their music. I guess that eviction got them changing their ways. But I spoke too soon. When I went to check my mail, I saw the neighbors outside arguing. I could only imagine what they were arguing about this time. Then as I made my way back into the house and sat down on the sofa, I heard my doorbell ring. It was Kimmey, the neighbor. When I answered the door, she tried to be nice and then asked if she could get our Wi-Fi password because their internet got turned off.

I tell her, "Rashad really doesn't like me giving the password out because it makes the internet go slow because of too many people using it."

She says, "Okay. I guess I will go to the store or something to get access." As she leaves, she looks back and says, "Before I go, I heard you be doing spells and stuff like that. Do you think you can help me with something?"

Reluctantly I say, "I don't know, it depends. What do you need help with?"

Kimmey then says, "I don't know if you heard but we have to move out by the end of the month. All the houses that we've looked at are too expensive or want deposits that we can't afford. So, I was thinking that you could do some magic to help us find a new place. I would be willing to pay you."

Listening to her story, I really wanted to say no thank you but since they are leaving and no longer going to be my problem, I say, "Okay I might be able to help." We sit on the porch, and she tells me, "We really need somewhere to go. Neither one of us is working right now, so money is tight. We are trying to get rental assistance, but they have a long waiting list."

I tell her, "I can help you secure a place, but I am not making any guarantees. You must also do your part too."

She says, "Ok. But before you do it, I just want to let you know, I am a Christian going woman. I don't want you to be making no packs with the devil for me."

I stand their stunned because that's the type of shit I hate. People always think what I do is the devil's work but at the same time their desperate for help, so they come to me. Unsure of if I wanted to help her, I just look at her for a minute before responding. I decided to let that slide and responded, "You don't have to worry about me making a pact for you and I don't believe in the devil. What I do is work with energy and herbs. Now if you want, I can do a spell for you tonight. Tell me your date of birth and full name. Once I have that I can do a ritual tonight for you to get a new place. But I make no guarantees and like I said you must do your part. You need to start looking for places and jobs tonight cause a house ain't just gonna fall in your lap."

Kimmey said, "Okay, I promise. I will look tonight but I don't have the internet so can I get the password?"

The nerve of this woman, still asking for the Wi-Fi password even after I promised to help her, people have no shame. Against my better judgement, I decide to give her the password. Afterall I can change it later.

I say, "Okay Kimmey, here is the password. And like I said look for houses and jobs or even apply for housing assistance. That way the universe will see that you are putting action towards your goals of getting a new house."

In a hurry to leave Kimmey says, "I told you I will start tonight and thanks for the password."

As she walks off, I think to myself that she has no idea that I am the one responsible for her moving out. I know she would be pissed if she found out I did a spell to make them move. But on the bright side I am helping her get a new place, so I say we are even. That night I set up my ritual for Kimmey and put all my energy into it because I need them to move far away from me.

About two days later while having my morning coffee I hear a knock at my door, it was Kimmey.

I opened the door and asked, “Hey Kimmey, do you need something?”

Smiling from ear to ear, she goes, “Girl I just want to thank you for your spell. We found a place to stay.”

“Oh, that’s great, I am glad I was able to help. Where are you moving to?”

“Girl you will never guess but we are moving to Florida.”

“Florida? How did that happen?”

“Yes, girl Florida. My grandmother lives there, and she called me yesterday saying how she was in the hospital. She said she is going to need someone to help her because she will not be able to walk for a couple of months. She was going to hire a nurse, but I told her I could help, and she said that having family there would be better. At first, she didn’t want my kids and husband to come but I told her about our housing situation, and I guess she felt bad and told me to bring them. She said as long as my husband gets a job, and the kids are good we can stay for however long we want since it’s just her.”

“Wow, I am shocked. I am glad it worked out for you.”

“Yea me too. And she lives like twenty minutes from the beach, so the kids are excited. I can’t believe things worked out so well. Thank you for helping me. I would pay you, but I am kinda low on funds being we gotta move in a couple of weeks.”

“Oh, don’t worry about it. I am just glad I could help.”

I go back into the house, happy as can be. Those people are finally getting out of my hair, and I feel even better since I helped them to get a new house to move to. I know I asked for them to move far away but I never knew it would be out of state. Damn I’m good.

When I came back into the kitchen, Rashad asked me, "What was that all about?"

Gleaming with pride I told him, "That was Kimmey, she was thanking me for helping them to find somewhere to stay."

He says, "I didn't know you were helping them but that's the least you can do. I knew you were capable of being a good witch."

I say, "Ha-ha very funny, but I don't care what you say, I am proud of myself. Everything worked out for the good in the end."

CHAPTER 3

SWEETENING SPELL

As the weeks went by, I eagerly waited for the neighbors to move out. Then finally the big day had come. When I pulled in the yard from picking up Amir from school, we saw the neighbors with their moving boxes. I got out of the car, looked across the street and waved at them. I stood outside watching Amir as he went to say good-bye to his friend across the street. As he made his way back, we watched the neighbors pull off in their moving truck. Like good neighbors we waved goodbye as they drove off to their new home in Florida. No one could tell but I was jumping for joy on the inside. I couldn't believe the neighbors from hell were really leaving. While I was on cloud nine, Amir seemed to be sad because he was losing his friend.

As we watched them drive away, I asked Amir, "Are you sad because your friend is moving away?"

Amir said, "Yea but I am sad because I had a bad day at school too."

I asked him, "Really, what happened?"

He replied, "My teacher Miss Mims keeps picking on me for no reason. I don't think she likes me. She always says I need to study more."

I tell him, "I'm sure she just wants you to do your best. Maybe I will call her and talk about it."

Shaking his head, Amir says, "No, Mommy, don't call her. I just want her to stop being mean to me."

I can't believe my son was having an issue with his teacher. He has always been a good student and consistently makes As and Bs, so I didn't understand why this teacher had such a problem with him.

When Rashad came home, I told him that Amir thought his teacher was being mean to him and to my surprise Rashad says, "Don't get any ideas to put a spell on his teacher."

Surprised by his response, I say, "What? Rashad, are you serious? The first thing that comes to your mind is to tell me not to do any spells. You really need to check yourself. And just to let you know if there's something that I can do to get my son to do better in school, I will do it. Spell or not."

Rashad then tells me, "Don't get offended, I wasn't trying to tell you what to do. I was just suggesting that we can talk to the teacher before you take matters into your own hands. You know how you do."

I then say, "No, Rashad, I don't know how I do. Why don't you tell me?"

Looking over at him for his response, he quickly says, "Ayanna, let's be real you know you're quick to put a spell on people, but I really didn't mean anything by it. I was just joking with you."

Still in defense mode, I say, "Hmm, yea right whatever. If you were joking you should have said that in the beginning, instead of acting like I cast spells on people for no reason."

Rashad then says, "Baby, I am not trying to start an argument I am just saying you're quick to put a spell on someone. I love you Ayanna, but you know it's the truth."

I roll my eyes and say, "Okay whatever, Rashad. I'm going to my room because you are really annoying me right now."

As I laid in the bed that night, I wondered what happened to my supportive husband who had my back? Instead of supporting me he's accusing me of putting spells on any and everybody. I don't know what has gotten into him, but I don't like it. I can't help but to think about putting a spell on his ass. He needs to chill and let me do what I do. Or maybe I'm tripping, and he was right. No, he's just getting an attitude but why? He was all supportive in me casting spells when he was on the receiving end like getting that promotion at work. He's been different ever since those ghetto ass neighbors moved out. I don't get it but whatever it is, I am not stopping my magic, point blank period. He will just have to get over it.

The next day, I called up my cousin Nisha to talk about Rashad. I usually don't talk about my relationship to others, but I had to vent to someone, and she was just the person I needed to talk to.

As soon as Nisha answers, I ask her, "What are you doing?"

Nisha says, "Nothing, what's up with you?"

Eager to let out my frustrations, I say, "Girl, last night Rashad really made me mad. Amir is having some issues with his teacher at school and when I told Rashad what happened he tells me, "Don't go putting a spell on the teacher." Like I just go around putting spells on people for no reason. That really pissed me off."

As I am telling her what happened, she laughs as usual. Then follows up with, "I can't believe he said that he usually doesn't even care about you doing spells. I wonder why he is acting like that?"

Agreeing with her, I say, "Yea me too. That's what has my mind wondering."

Nisha then says, "Well maybe he has something going on at work or something that's making him act like that. But you're right, he is usually laid back and cool when it comes to your magic."

I say, "Exactly. That's the same thing I was thinking. It was all good, when he was asking, "Baby help me get a promotion or what can I do to get me a good bonus this year," he didn't mind my spells then."

Nisha says, "Maybe he's just mad cause you're not helping him and your helping other people. Men can be jealous."

I tell Nisha, "I don't know what it is, but I don't like it. But I will have to deal with him later. Amir just came in from school. I will call you back because I want to see how it went with his teacher today."

Nisha says, "Okay. Call me later. Bye."

I hang up the phone and say hi to Amir and ask him, "How was school?"

"It was okay. My teacher was mean again."

"What? Why, what happened today?"

"Miss Mims told me I need to practice my writing more and that I was not using complete sentences. But some other kids in class did the same thing but she didn't say anything to them."

"Okay well that's the last time that will happen. I am going to call her. On second thought, let's make her something. They say you get more bees with honey and that's what we will do."

Since Rashad didn't want me putting spells on people, I will show him why they call me a kitchen witch.

Amir then asks me, "What do you mean mom? What should I make her?"

I tell him, "Don't worry, I will make her some sweet treats."

While Rashad told me not to put a spell on the teacher, he didn't say anything about making her something. I wouldn't dare tell my husband about what I am going to do but this is kitchen witching at its finest. I am going to cook up Miss Mims some cookies and put my spell in the ingredients. Some sweets to make her sweet to my son.

I bring out my cookbook and decide to make Snickerdoodle cookies. They have all the ingredients that contain spices to make someone sweet. Cinnamon, sugar, and a dash of vanilla. As I gather my ingredients and mix them together, I give each ingredient an assignment. The sugar to sweeten up Miss Mims, the vanilla to make her love my son, and cinnamon to show favor and luck for Amir. I mix them up and visualize Miss Mims being nice and kind to Amir. I speak success over the batter for Amir to get good grades in school. As I finish mixing and before placing them in the oven, I speak a simple rhyme for my spell. I say, "With every cookie that Miss Mims will eat, she will show favor to Amir and be sweet." I know these cookies will do the trick and get Amir on her good side.

When Rashad came home, he came into the kitchen and asked me what I was doing. I simply said, "I am baking some cookies."

Amir then comes in and says, "We are going to give some to Miss Mims."

To my surprise Rashad says, "Oh that's good. See you can get what you want by being nice and sweet and not just casting spells."

I say, "Yea you're right I told Amir you get more bees with honey." To his surprise I had my spell imbedded in the cookies and he would never know it. I guess I would have to do this more often since he was against me casting spells.

The next day, I remind Amir to bring the cookies to his teacher and if he has any issues to let me know. When he makes it home from school, I ask him how his day went.

He says, "Mommy, Miss Mims started being nice like you said. She was happy that I decided to make her cookies. She said no one else has ever brought her gifts."

With a smile on my face, I say, "Oh that's wonderful. See I told you it was a good idea."

Amir then says, "Miss Mims also wanted you to call her."

I say, "Really, okay. I will call her now to see what she has to say."

I am surprised that Amir's teacher wants to talk being that everything went well. I guess I will find out what she wants. I pick up my phone and call Miss Mims.

"Hello, Miss Mims, this is Ayanna. Amir's mother."

Miss Mims says, "Oh yes. I wanted to speak with you about Amir. Well first, I want to say thank you for the cookies. They were delicious."

"Oh, you're welcome, I am glad you liked them."

"Yes. I told Amir that no student has ever brought me cookies. That was so sweet of him. Now regarding his grades, I did want to say that I know I have been kind of hard on him, but I just know he has so much potential. I really want him to live up to his greatness. And I want to keep it real with you, being one of the only black students in my class, I want him to be the best, that's why I am so hard on him. But I know he doesn't see it that way, so I wanted to speak with you and apologize if I made him feel bad."

I tell Miss Mims, "Yes, he was actually thinking you didn't like him."

"No that is far from the truth. I just know what he is capable of and want him to be at the top of the class that's why I push him. But from now on I am changing my approach, I will be nicer because I know he is young and thinks I am picking on him. Actually, I want him to join the afterschool program where he can get more involved with math and science projects so that he is not left behind. I see so many black children who have potential and I want him to thrive."

"Okay I will let him know. I am glad we had this talk and cleared that up."

"Yea me too. And thanks again for those cookies. I will have to get your recipe so I can make some at home."

I laughed and said, "Okay." Deep down inside I knew I could give her the recipe, but she wouldn't be able to make the cookies like I did.

After getting off the phone I spoke with Amir and Rashad about the phone call.

Amir was glad that his teacher really liked him, and Rashad swore my cookies did the trick.

To my surprise Rashad said, "See I told you baby. Being nice gets a better outcome than spells. Don't you think?"

I smiled and said, "Yea if you say so." I wanted to tell him what I had done but I had to keep that a secret. He would probably be mad, but it got Amir on his teacher's good side, and she is willing to help him be at the top of his class. I call that a win in my book.

CHAPTER 4

LOVE SPELL

While I felt good about my most recent success with getting the neighbors gone and sweetening up Amir's teacher, I kept getting a nagging feeling about my husband. I don't know what was up with his holier than thou attitude about me casting spells. Something was off with him, but I couldn't put my finger on it. I needed some advice from my fellow witches, so I decided to meet up with them.

As I sat in the restaurant waiting for Drea and Jewel, the waiter brought me a glass of wine that I did not order. I tell the waiter, "Excuse me but I didn't order this."

He said, "I know its compliments of the gentleman at the bar. He wanted to ask if you were married."

Shocked, I looked up at the bar and it was a sexy man sitting there. He had such smooth dark chocolate skin and a white pearly smile to match. Not only that, but he also had long dreads pulled back like he belonged on an Island in Jamaica. All I could think was now I know how Stella got her groove back, because this man was fine. Even though he was fine, and I was thoroughly impressed, I smiled and told the waiter, "Please let him know that I am married but thank him for the drink."

As the girls came in and sat down, I couldn't wait to tell them about that sexy, fine ass man at the bar.

I asked them, "Do y'all see that man at the bar with the dreads? He sent me a glass of wine."

"What? He is fine. You must have a love spell on you or something," Drea said.

I say, "Why does it have to be a love spell? When you got it, you got it."

Drea then says, “Yea you’re right but you’re married so leave the men to me.”

I laughed and told them, “Honestly, I wish my husband would look at me like that. For the last couple of weeks, he has been such a prude when it comes to my magic.”

“Not Rashad. I thought he was all for it. Especially when you said you helped him get a promotion,” said Jewel.

I said, “Exactly. That’s what I said. But now he’s like everything doesn’t need a spell.”

“The hell it don’t! Not a day goes by where I don’t use a spell or some type of magic. Hell, magic is my life and I dare someone to tell me to give it up,” said Drea.

“You’re right about that Drea. I don’t know what I would do if I had a man who was against my magic. That’s probably why I don’t have a man right now,” said Jewel.

We all laughed, and I said, “Y’all are crazy. But I am serious what can I do to get him to stop criticizing me? I mean every time I even hint at doing a spell, he gets up tight about it.”

Jewel says, “You know what we should do. A love and attraction ritual. Drea, you need a man, Ayanna you need more love from your man and well when it comes to me, I just love, love.”

“Jewel, you need a man too. Don’t act like you don’t,” Drea hollered out.

Laughing Jewel says, “Maybe I do, it has been a while since I been on a date. So, that’s it we’re doing the ritual.”

Jewel pulls out her phone and starts with a list of things that we will need for the ritual.

By the end of the night, we had a full-on love and attraction ritual that we were going to perform. I will admit that the ritual gave me hope about rekindling the spark in my relationship since Rashad has been so standoffish lately.

As the weekend came, we all met at Jewel's house to carry out the ritual. We decided to do the ritual on Friday to honor Venus, the Goddess of Love. Drea being the self-proclaimed Spirit Witch, told us that the days of the week were named after Gods and Goddesses and Friday was for Venus. Since Friday is the day of love, it will give our ritual extra power.

We assembled our ritual with roses, red and pink candles and herbs associated with love. We cleansed the space with sage and each of us wore a rose quartz crystal for love. We stood in a circle holding hands and chanting, "Bring me love, just like the Goddess Venus from above."

As we finished with the ritual, I couldn't help but to think how much in love my husband would be with me. A little part of me kind of wondered if I really needed to do this. I know my husband loved me and maybe I just needed to talk to him but it's too late now. I have put my love in the hands of the universe.

Since the love ritual I hadn't seen any changes in Rashad, but I did notice an increase in attention from men. From the grocery store to the gas station, I had men telling me how pretty I was, and some were even asking me for my number. I guess the spell was working but not how I expected.

Another additional outcome that I didn't expect was my ex-boyfriend Jayvon sending me a message on social media. I was surprised to say the least, it had been almost five years since I even spoke to him or saw him. Jayvon was a good man but when we were together, we were young and didn't know any better. I am not going to lie if it wasn't for him getting his ex-girlfriend pregnant all those years ago, we would probably be married. I can't believe I am even thinking about this man. Our relationship was the off and on-again thing, but it was real love, and I could not deny that. I wondered what he wanted with me since he was happily married at this point in his life. Against my better judgement I decided to open his message. Opening his message made me feel as if I was opening pandora's box. Let me just click the open button and see what he has to say.

The message said, "Hey beautiful. I had a dream about you, so I just wanted to see how you were doing."

Wow, did he really think I was falling for that lame line. But I decided to reply.

My response was, "Hey. I am good. That must have been some dream. Hope you are doing good also."

I can't believe I replied to him. Being a married woman, I felt guilty for responding but then again there is nothing wrong with sending an innocent message. Later that day we messaged each other constantly. I will admit Jayvon always had a great sense of humor and charm that I loved. It reminded me when we were younger and how we used to talk and laugh on the phone for hours.

As the days went by, we stopped the messages and started to talk on the phone. While talking Jayvon tells me that he was going to be in my area this weekend.

I say, "Really, you just happen to be in my city?"

He says, "Yea, there is a club that I am thinking about investing in. I am trying to diversify my investments; the owner is looking for a couple of other business partners so I think a club would be a good way to make additional money."

I tell him, "Well, you always had a great mind for business. I hope it works out for you."

He says, "Yea me too, but I want you to meet me while I'm there?"

I hesitate and say, "Um I don't know Jayvon. I am a married lady and you're married too."

He then says, "I know but were just friends. Ain't nothing wrong with seeing an old friend, right?"

I tell him, "I don't know if my husband would like that and what about your wife. I don't think she would like you seeing another woman, especially me."

He laughed and said, “You know she has always been jealous of you.”

I say, “She shouldn’t be jealous. You did marry her, so she got the last laugh.”

Jayvon says, “Now you know I wanted to be with you, but you were tripping. All those times I confessed my love to you, but you kept running from me.”

I laughed and said, “Whatever. You’re the same old Jayvon trying to run game on me.”

He says, “Naw Ayanna, I am serious. I want to see you for real cause I do miss you. Just meet me for a drink and that will be it. I promise.”

Reluctantly, I say, “Okay. I will meet you. Please don’t make me regret my decision.”

In a confident tone Jayvon says, “Trust me, you won’t.”

When Saturday came around, I couldn’t believe I was going to meet up with Jayvon. My husband would probably kill me if he knew I was going to see an ex-boyfriend. But I will just have to keep that a secret.

As I walked into the hotel’s restaurant, I saw Jayvon at the bar. I must admit he still looked good. He had the most beautiful brown chocolate skin and nice soft lips to go with it. He had on a fitted shirt that showed off his nicely shaped chest and arms. As I greeted him, he stood up and gave me a hug. The smell of his cologne made me feel so good and warm in his arms. If I wasn’t married, I probably would have asked for a kiss, but I would never let him know that.

As we sat down, Jayvon asked me how I was doing but I wanted to get down to the real conversation.

So, I boldly said, “Let’s skip all the pleasantries. I want to know why you got me here meeting with you?”

He says, "What do you mean? I told you I wanted to see you. And don't be questioning me, you're the one that came up in here with your short skirt on showing off those pretty brown thighs that I used to rub on. Not to mention you got that red lipstick on that you know I always loved on you. And don't try to act like you forgot."

As I tilted my head down and smiled, I said, "Oh yea I remember you did used to say that."

He then says, "I know you didn't forget what I like so don't even try it. Besides that, what's been up with you? I heard you're a witch now."

Shocked, I ask, "Who told you that?"

He said, "My cousin, Chris."

I said, "Should have known it was Chris. Chris always did have a big mouth and be all up in everybody's business. But anyways if you must know I call myself a Kitchen Witch. So, if you do me wrong, I might have to put a hex on you."

Jayvon says, "Damn it's like that. I have nothing but love for you, Ayanna and you know that. But I ain't gonna lie, you do look good tho'. I'm really trying to be respectful but I'm fantasizing about how good it would feel to kiss those lips again."

Blushing, I shake my head in disbelief and say, "You need to stop you're married and so am I."

He says, "I know but you know you have always been the love of my life."

I say, "Yea right, Jayvon. You're about to piss me off with that because you're the one who went and got another girl pregnant and then married her. So please stop with that bullshit. You're taking me back to a time that I wanted to forget."

Jayvon says, "See you're getting all mad because you know it's true. And don't you dare put it all on me. You're the one who didn't want a serious relationship but then you went and got married yourself. You didn't know what you wanted."

Getting annoyed, I say, "You know what Jayvon let's stop bringing up the past. I didn't come here for that."

He then says, "Hmm. So, tell me what did you come here for?"

I look at him and say, "Umm not what you think apparently. I wanted to see you and see how you were doing."

Jayvon then grabs my hand and says, "Okay now that you saw me, let's get some alone time and go up to my room. I promise I won't try anything unless you want."

I gently pull my hand away and say, "Yea right, I am going to pass on that offer. You must think I'm slow or something? You're really trying it tonight."

He then commanded, "Let's go to the pool where we can relax."

I accepted the offer to go to the pool. We sit on the edge of the pool reminiscing about old times. I must admit, it had turned out to be a great night. To be honest when we dated all those years ago, we would always somehow find ourselves in a hotel bed but tonight was different. Just two friends hanging out but that was until he decided to splash water in my face. I became mad but as he got a towel and wiped the water off my face, his hand slightly touched my cheek and we looked into each other's eyes. Then you guessed it, we engaged in a passionate kiss that seemed to last for about five minutes. I couldn't believe this was happening and not to mention how good it felt. As our lips parted, he asked me to come up to his room, but I knew better. I declined and told him that I had to go home.

I made it home and as I walked into my room, I saw my husband fast asleep. Looking at my husband made me have remorse for kissing another man. However, I can't help but to think how good it felt having someone compliment me and tell me how good I look unlike how my husband was treating me. But that was no reason for me to kiss another man. I couldn't believe after all these years of being faithful I let Jayvon kiss me.

The next day I felt so much guilt, I had to confess my sins. Since I couldn't and wouldn't ever tell Rashad, I decided to call Drea to confide in.

Soon as Drea picks up the phone, I start on my rant and say, "Drea, y'all must have messed up that spell because I am attracting everyone but my damn husband."

She laughed and said, "What are you talking about, Ayanna? Are you getting too much attention?"

I say, "Girl, yes because I ended up meeting with my ex, Jayvon and we kissed. I keep reliving that kiss in my head. I literally can't stop thinking about it."

She laughs and says, "It was that good huh?"

I say, "I hate to admit but yes. He just has that effect on me. After last night he keeps texting me, saying he loves me and should have married me. Now he wants me to see him this weekend and go to one of the clubs that he is thinking about investing in. You think I should go?"

Drea says, "Now didn't you just say how you regret meeting him. I don't know him, but it seems like he is just trying to get you back or better yet get you back in his bed. Trust me I've seen this before. He's a married man who feels like his marriage is getting stale and wants something new. And that new thing is you. You must have put it on him back in the day."

Laughing, I tell her, "I can't argue with that, but I think I may meet him. Just to see him again. I mean we have fun and I genuinely like him as a friend."

Drea responds, "Okay keep telling yourself that. When he got you in his hotel room don't come calling me."

I say, "Ha. I am serious he is fun to hang out with plus it's not like I can't control myself."

Drea says, "You know what, you're going to do what you want anyway. So just do it."

Drea was right, I did want to see him, and I had already made up my mind that I was going to meet him. Honestly, it's not like my husband was paying me any attention these days. Rashad had already told me that he was going out this weekend with his coworkers to God knows where. All I know is that he wasn't going to be with me. In a sudden case of loneliness, I text Jayvon and tell him I will meet up with him this weekend.

When the weekend came, I pulled up to the hotel and let Jayvon know that I was downstairs. He tells me to come to his room, but I stay firm and say no. I tell him I will stay in the lobby. Jayvon comes down and we have some drinks before going to the club.

While riding in the car he places his hand on my thigh while he drives. For some odd reason I didn't tell him to move his hand. I guess deep down I liked it and it brought back old feelings that I had for him. I looked over at him and smiled while touching his hand. I knew this was wrong, but it felt so good. Finally, we make our way to the club. Before we go inside, Jayvon warns me that people at this club are out there. And boy he wasn't wrong. As we walk through the club, I see women with see through dresses on and even lingerie. I ask him, "Is this a strip club or something?"

He said "No" but the way they are dressed says otherwise. He tells me to relax and that I will like it.

As we walk through the club I see people of all ages, sizes, and races. Then a lady approaches me and asks if I would like to dance and I politely say no. I don't have anything against lesbians, but as they used to say back in the day, I am strictly, dickly. Then suddenly everything made sense as I see two half naked women kissing with a half-naked man sitting between them. This was a Swingers Club. I knew the club's name seemed familiar to me. This club has been in the news because people wanted to shut it down. I turn around and scream to Jayvon, "Is this a Swingers Club?"

With a grin on his face he says, "Yea, I thought you would like it."

Over the loud music I hollered at Jayvon, "What the hell, I am not a swinger. I am leaving!"

I run through the club and find my way to the door. He comes right behind me begging me to stay.

I say, "Jayvon, why in the hell did you not tell me this was a Swingers Club? And not only that why did you think I would like something like this?"

He says, "I'm sorry, I thought you were down, we did have that kiss last time. And come on now Ayanna, I know you're a freak. Remember all the things we used to do when we were together. Plus, me and my wife go to places like this all the time so I thought you would be down too."

"Well, I am not down with swinging," I said.

He then goes, "Okay well if you are not into swinging, we can swap partners. You told me your husband doesn't pay you any attention so maybe he wants something new. That way me and you can get together without our partners getting mad."

Shocked by his response, I tell him, "Boy you are crazy. I can't believe this is really happening. You need to take me to the hotel so I can get my car and go home."

After realizing that I would not go back in the club and that I wasn't down with his new lifestyle, he took me back to the hotel. I got out the car without saying a word and I drove myself home.

I walked into my house and took a long hot shower. I couldn't sleep due to reliving what just happened over and over in my head. To hell with this love and attraction spell. The universe really has a way of giving you what you want.

CHAPTER 5
TRUTH TEA

Thinking about last night's craziness, I decided to call Drea and tell her about my fun filled night.

"Hey Drea. What are you up to?"

Drea said, "Nothing just doing some laundry. What's up with you? How was your date?"

I said, "That's exactly why I called you. I had to wait for Rashad to leave because I certainly don't want him to hear this."

I get up and check to make sure his car is gone before I start to talk. "Now about last night, this boy had the nerve to take me to a Swingers Club."

Drea screamed, "What! Are you serious?"

I said, "Yes. You heard me right, a damn swingers club and didn't even have the nerve to tell me beforehand. I only realized what it was once I saw people kissing and damn near having sex with each other. This was the club he wanted to invest in. Not to mention he also told me him and his wife were into swinging and wanted to potentially swap partners with me and my husband."

Astonished by Ayanna's confession, Drea says, "Girl I am totally shocked. If you could see my face right now. I didn't even know black people were into that swinging stuff. That's crazy."

I say, "Yea, I know, and I don't want to be involved in any of that. After last night, I told him we're done. I never want to talk to him again. Better yet I blame you and Jewel because this never would've happened if it wasn't for that damn love and attraction spell."

Drea says, "Girl, say what you want. I have met about two men since then. And anyways you had no business doing it since you already got a man. A good man at that."

I agree and say, "Yea you're right. I'm just going to have a heart to heart with Rashad so we can get back on track because I see ain't nothing better out there in those streets."

"Yep, do that and no more swinging," Drea said as she laughed.

I then say, "Now tell me about these men you met?"

Drea gives me the tea on the men she met and says, "One is a Police Officer that I met at the gas station the other day and the other is a Barber. I like them both, but I can't date two men, so I need to let one of them go."

I tell her, "Girl please, the more the better. Let me stop I don't want to influence you but when I was single I had about two or three in rotation."

Drea says, "Ayanna, you are crazy, but I don't have enough time for two. Actually, I have to get off the phone because I have an early lunch date with Mr. Officer."

I tell Drea bye since she seemed to be in a rush to meet her new guy. After I got off the phone, I sat there thinking about how I could have potentially ruined my marriage by messing with Jayvon. I can't believe I was that stupid to go out with him. What the hell was I thinking. That's the thing I wasn't thinking, just mad because my husband isn't being his usual self. I need to talk to him about it so he can go back to the nice and sweet man he used to be.

He must have known I was thinking about him, because all of a sudden Rashad came in the room.

He looked around and said, "Hey Baby. What are you doing?"

I said, "Nothing. I just got off the phone. What are you up to?"

He says, "Me and Amir were just out washing the car. Amir is outside playing with the cat."

Getting the courage to talk to him about our issues, I say, "Okay. Well maybe we can talk about something. I feel like you've been acting different especially when it comes to my magic and spells."

He says, "I don't know what you mean. I am the same old Rashad who you married. But I will say sometimes you get so caught up with your spells you don't have time for me."

I say, "Now Rashad, you know that's not true. I feel like that's how you do me. You're the one always staying late at work and then criticizing me whenever I do a spell."

Rashad then says, "You know I have been working lots of hours since my boss left. I have been doing his job along with mines. I won't have to stay so late once my new boss gets up to speed. Now as for the spells, you do go overboard. Sometimes you just need to chill and let things play out instead of always interfering."

Not wanting to argue, I say, "Well maybe you're right but I miss our time together."

He says, "Just be patient. I won't be working like this all the time."

I say, "Okay. I love you."

Before walking out the room he says, "I love you too."

After Rashad left, I sat there thinking about how much I did love my husband. I couldn't believe how I was about to risk it all for my ex. That would have been a big mistake.

As the days went by, I still couldn't understand how Rashad had the nerve to say I neglect him. I cook almost every day, wash his clothes, and never deny him sex but I neglect him. The nerve of him. I know marriages have their ups and downs, so I guess this is the down part.

Sitting here with our cat, KitKat, I rub her black fur as she purrs. She truly understands me and is always there for me. Not that I don't have support but when it lacks from your husband it really hurts. I just have to be patient and ride out this down patch.

As I sit there my phone rings and it was Drea. She wanted to talk about her current love interests. As we talk, she tells me she wants to do a spell on the guy that she is dating. I tell her we can meet and talk at her place. I definitely can't have anyone over here doing spells since Rashad was not feeling my magic right now.

I meet up at her house and we talk about her two lovers. As we talk, she says, "I like Damon the Police Officer, but he is hiding something. He told me he has a child but for some reason he doesn't want me to visit his house. He keeps saying his roommate is messy and doesn't want me to see his house."

I tell her, "Girl, now you know damn well that's code for I am living with my girlfriend, baby momma or wife."

Drea says, "Yea I know but he promised me he was single, and it was only a roommate situation."

I tell her, "Well ain't nothing but one way to find out. Let's get to the bottom of it with a truth spell."

She says, "I got everything we need. His picture, some rosemary, and my lemon oil, this makes the best truth potion. Just let me go get my candles and we can start."

Miss Jay had taught us this truth spell so I knew it would work.

When she comes back with the candles, we take the herbs and oils and place them around the candle. I take his picture and place it beneath the candle. Drea takes her spell and we read it aloud while holding hands. We say, "Show me the real so the truth will be revealed." We repeat this for about five minutes and let the candle burn.

Once done we go into the kitchen and drink some tea. After drinking the tea, I tell Drea, "I don't know why you are doing this spell, you already know he is hiding something. Instead of the truth spell you need to fix him some truth tea."

Drea goes, "That's a perfect idea, I will make some when he comes over to my house. The truth is going to come out. I don't know how or when, but I need the truth."

I say, "The truth will come out just like my situation with Jayvon. I can't believe I almost cheated on Rashad. I know I complain but Rashad is a good man."

Drea says, "You are right Ayanna, but everyone is not as lucky to have a good man like Rashad. Damon has the potential to be a good man, but he is lying to me about something."

I say, "We shall see. But it's getting late. Let me get home to my family before Rashad says I'm neglecting them. Call me later okay."

As I went to bed that night, I had the most vivid dream, and it was pertaining to Drea's man.

I call up Drea and tell her about my dream.

I tell her, "You will never guess what I dreamed about last night."

Drea asked, "What?"

I tell her, "I saw Damon in my dream, and someone was telling him, "You need to stop fooling these women." It was an older lady saying this along with calling him a liar. Maybe that was his mom trying to get him to come clean."

Drea says, "Well that confirms my suspicion that he is hiding something. I might just confront him about it so I can stop obsessing over it. I can't wait until he comes over, he should actually be here in about an hour. You're dream already gave me some information, but the tea is going to make everything come out. Let me get my truth tea ready. I will call you back and give you an update."

I would love to be a fly on the wall at Drea's house right now because I know it's going to go down.

At Drea's House

Drea liked Damon but she knew the truth had to come out. Damon texted Drea and said he was on his way. Drea made her way to the kitchen and finished up making her batch of truth tea.

As soon as Damon comes in, Drea hugged him and said, "Hey Baby, you look good."

Damon said, "Thank you. You look good yourself," as he gave Drea a kiss. After the kiss his phone rang, and he went to the other room.

When he came back Drea asked, "Who was that?"

Damon said, "Drea, you're being nosey. It was just my job; they need me down at the station tonight."

Drea then says, "Calm down I was just asking a simple question. Why don't you sit down and let me get you some tea."

While he drinks the tea, Drea casually says, "Guess what? My friend had a dream about you."

He says, "Oh really."

Drea says, "Yea, she said it was about you hiding something."

Then suddenly Damon starts breathing hard and gets defensive and says, "Oh so one of your witch bitch friends tells you something and you believe them."

Seemingly upset at Damon's response, Drea says, "First of all don't refer to my friend as a bitch and if you would tell the truth, it wouldn't be a problem."

He then says, "I got to go to the bathroom. I will be back."

Under her breath, Drea says, "I guess the tea went straight through him." She also notices that he left his phone. She thinks now is the time for her to get down to the bottom of his secrets. As she sits there debating if she should try to unlock his phone, a text comes in.

She opens the text and reads it. The text is from Davis Security confirming his 8 o'clock shift for tonight. Surprised by this, Drea wonders why a Security Company would be texting him when he works for the police. She thinks this must be a part time job cause he never mentioned it.

Eager to confront him, Drea waits for him to come out of the bathroom. Once he comes back to the living room she asks, “What is Davis Security?”

Damon looks down and sees his phone screen unlocked. He grabs the phone from the sofa and yells, “Drea why in the hell were you in my phone?”

Drea yells back and asks, “Who the hell are you talking to like that?”

Damon says, “I am talking to you and why are you all up in my business like you’re my wife or something!”

Drea says, “You know what Damon you can get the hell out but before you do you owe me the truth.”

He then said, “Well if you want the truth here you go, I ain’t no damn police officer. I am a security guard and the woman I live with is my momma. So, there you go with your damn insecure ass.”

Surprised by his confession, Drea says, “How dare you call me insecure when you’re the one living with your momma and then lying about your profession. Get your lying ass out of my house.”

As he left out Drea was completely shocked. She wondered why he lied about his job and even saying his momma was his roommate. She then thought everything he told her could have been a lie.

Sitting on the sofa, shocked and confused Drea called Ayanna to tell her what happened. Ayanna could not stop laughing but she assured Drea that it was better that she found out now about his lies rather than later.

Drea agreed and said, “Yea I dodged a bullet with that one. I just wonder how long he was going to keep up with his lies?”

Ayanna said, “Girl, I don’t know but he seemed like a compulsive liar. On another note, we know our spell worked. The truth came out fast. We did a good job on that one.”

Drea said, “I guess there’s a silver lining with every situation, huh. But let me get off the phone so I can sage my place and get his lying energy out of my house.”

CHAPTER 6
WORK WIFE

I can't believe that Drea's police officer boyfriend turned out to be a liar. I was dying laughing when she told me what happened even after we got off the phone. As I sat there laughing to myself, Rashad walked in and asked what was so funny. I tell him about Drea's fake police officer boyfriend, and he laughed too. I enjoyed laughing with Rashad, it seemed like we were back to our old fun-loving relationship. Then all of a sudden, he tells me that he has a company party coming up next week.

I say, "Rashad, if you knew about this last month why didn't you tell me then? It's not that I don't want to go I just like to be prepared that's all."

Rashad then says, "I'm sorry, I actually didn't plan on going myself however, my new boss wanted me to come so I decided to go."

I say, "Okay. That means that I will finally get to meet the new boss who has you staying late."

He says, "Yep. I am sure you will like her."

I say, "Her? Your boss is a woman?"

He says, "Yea. What's wrong with that?"

I say, "Nothing Rashad. I just assumed your boss was a man that's all. You never talk about your boss so how was I supposed to know."

Rashad says, "Oh ok but I know you will like her, she's cool."

I tell him, "Hmm. Sounds like you're the one who likes her."

Rolling his eyes, Rashad goes, "Oh there you go. Are you jealous?"

With a serious look on my face, I say, "No."

Even though I said no something deep down inside of me was jealous. Who was this woman that was spending so much time with my husband? Better yet what did she look like and how close were they? I guess I would find out soon enough.

The night of the party came, and I was ready to meet this new boss. I decided to wear my black dress with gold jewelry and proudly wear my diamond wedding band. I don't know why I felt like I had something to prove to a woman that I never met but my intuition was telling me to be on the lookout.

We arrive at the party and greet Rashad's co-workers and then go get a drink. While at the bar, I hear Rashad say, "Oh there goes my boss. Do you want to meet her?"

I say, "Not really but okay, if I must."

Rashad goes, "Don't act like that Baby. She's cool."

We walk over to his mystery boss. She is wearing a red tight strapless dress with her hair wrapped tightly in a high bun. Wearing red, I already knew she wanted attention but from who? As we walked over to her, I could see her smile when my husband approached her.

He said, "Hi Janelle. This is my wife, Ayanna."

His boss, Janelle, says, "Oh, hello Rashad, and it's nice to meet you, Ayanna. It's good to meet you after seeing your picture so many times. You're a lucky woman to be married to Rashad, he is one of the best members on my team."

I say, "Really, thank you. Are you married Janelle?"

Janelle says, "No, I'm not married. I was engaged twice but didn't quite make it to the vows. However, there is a joke around the office that Rashad is my work husband."

I look over at Rashad and say, "Really, is that right? You're her work husband?"

With a half-smile he says, "That's what everyone in the office says. You know how people joke around."

Janelle then interrupts and says, "Don't be mad at Rashad it's just a joke. Plus, I only have him for eight hours, but you have him for a lifetime."

I tell her, "Yea you're right I do but you have him more than eight hours because from what he says you have him working overtime."

Janelle says, "Oh yes don't be mad at me. Being new I need him to help me with a lot of the new accounts. I need his expertise but I will be up to speed in no time so you can have your man back."

I smile and say, "Okay, well that's good to hear. I better go get me another glass of wine it seems like it's going to be a long night."

I sashay my way to the bar and order a glass of red wine. While standing there I see Rashad still talking with Janelle. Now I see why he was staying late. He was probably over there trying to suck up to his boss or better yet was she sucking up to him. We will be having a conversation about this later.

As the night went on, I watched Janelle like a hawk. She was pretty and could have any man she wanted. That made me wonder why she would go after a married man and seemed so proud to be called his "Work Wife."

That term really rubbed me the wrong way. After the evening ended, I questioned Rashad on his relationship with Janelle. He swore it was only business.

Even though I believed him, I told him, "You seemed a little too friendly with her, especially with that work husband and wife stuff."

Breaking his silence he says, "Look, I am going to be honest; sometimes I do bring her coffee or lunch, but I am just being friendly. When she first started, she did ask me to go out with her and show her around the town."

I say, "What! And you're just now telling me this?"

Rashad says, "It's not a big deal, I don't think she knew I was married then."

I say, “Oh I am sure she knew. She can see your wedding band. That will tell her your off limits.”

Defending his boss, Rashad says, “I was quick to tell her I was married so I recommended someone else on the team to take her out. One of the other ladies on the team even asked her but she said she liked my vibe. But I told her if I took her around the town, I would have to bring you. You know I would never disrespect or cheat on you in any way.”

“That’s good to know and I am glad I can trust you, but I can’t trust Janelle.”

“Well don’t go getting any crazy ideas in your head. She’s a cool girl, just a little flirty.”

“Okay I will chill for now but if she ever tries to come at you again, you better let me know.”

The next day I start to think about the conversation I had with Rashad. I couldn’t believe he conveniently forgot to tell me about his encounter with his flirty boss. While he was not at fault that Janelle needed to be stopped and taught a lesson about going after married men.

I decided to talk the situation over with Jewel, but she brought up my encounter with my ex-boyfriend. Even though I felt that she should see my side of things, she did have a point. I shouldn’t be mad at Rashad because I was guilty in my own ways. But it wasn’t Rashad I was mad at; it was that overly friendly boss. I knew what I had to do to get her away from my husband.

Jewel asked me, “Ayanna, what are you going to do?”

I tell Jewel, “You know what I am going to do. Like Miss Jay says, for every situation, there is a spell for it. Plus all my life I been using the Michelle Obama approach and taking the high road. I want to be like Lil Jon and the Eastside Boys and get low sometimes! With the help of magic, I’m going to put that bitch in her place.”

Jewel says, “Okay, I have your back no matter what and I won’t judge you, just be careful.”

I knew my husband would not want me to do a spell on his boss, but this needed to be done. You don’t come after a woman’s husband and get away with it. I then go searching for the best spell I could find for my situation. After searching I found a separation spell that seemed to be very powerful.

While Rashad was at work, I found all of my herbs, candles, and crystals. I also found Janelle on social media where I was able to print out a picture of her. I placed her picture under my candles and chanted “Leave my man alone, out his life I command you to be gone.” I chanted this until I became dizzy and almost fainted. I must have really put my energy into this spell.

I sat there for a minute trying to process why I was so angry knowing I had gone after a married man myself. Maybe I felt guilty because I almost cheated and perhaps this could be karma coming for me. Since I felt dizzy, I decided to go to my room and lay down. After waking up from my nap, I got a phone call from Rashad. I hope he is not coming home early because I don’t want him to see my spell for his “work wife”.

I answer the phone and say, “Hello?”

“Hey Baby. I wanted to call you because I am going to be late getting home tonight. I got a call that Janelle was in the hospital, she was in a car accident. She has no family here, so she told them to call me. I will call you back when I know more.”

“Okay I hope it’s not serious. Let me know something when you get there.”

Damn all I could think was that spell worked fast. Even though I wanted her to stay away I never met for her to get into an accident. But the dark side of me thinks that’s what she gets for messing with my man, plus, the accident didn’t seem serious. I know that was probably wrong of me, but the Universe doesn’t tell us how karma is going to be served.

Later I got a call from Rashad, and he said that Janelle was okay, and she just had a broken arm. That meant that she was going to be working from home from now on and would not be in the office with my husband. Only her assistant would be helping her from home.

I know I should have felt bad for her, but that accident was payback for her going after a married man. However, on the upside I am glad my spell worked so fast and gave me exactly what I wanted which was for her to stay away from my man.

While I was not exactly proud of what I did, it had to be done. She would not take no for an answer. Since Jewel told me not to do the spell, I decided not to call her to tell her what happened. The only person with a dark side like me was my cousin Nisha. I decided to call her and gloat about my spell's success.

"Hey Nisha. What's Up?"

Nisha answers and says, "Nothing girl. I haven't talked to you in a while."

I say, "Yea well you know me I've just been chilling."

Knowing me well, Nisha says, "Just chilling huh, it sounds like you been up to something."

I tell her, "To be honest I did a spell on Rashad's new boss because she was flirting with him. And not only that she had the nerve to call him her work husband."

Nisha says, "What! I knew that made you angry."

I say, "Yep. Sure did and I did a spell to get her gone and guess what happened."

Nisha asked, "What?"

I tell her, "She got into a car accident and has to work from home now, away from my husband."

“Damn girl that was good. She won’t mess with your husband anymore.”

I say, “You got that right.”

Nisha says, “You’re getting really good with your spells.”

I say, “Oh here we go, what spell do you need me to do for you?”

“Well since you asked. I got a little issue with my boyfriend and his baby momma. She is trying to keep his kids from him. What can we do to make sure he keeps joint custody? He has court coming up next week.”

I say, “Hmm. I don’t know too much about court cases, but I can do a little research.”

Nisha says, “Well research and let me know. She is claiming that he is not fit because he works a late shift, and she is trying to get more child support. She is a mess.”

I tell Nisha, “Well text me her name and your boyfriend’s name and I will work on something.”

She says, “Thank you so much. I told him if anybody can help to secure a victory it would be you. I am glad you called.”

I start my research on the court case spell and Rashad walks in. He tells me his boss is getting better, but he had the nerve to say that I must have manifested her accident. I look at him and say, “Rashad, how dare you accuse me of causing an accident. The universe must have known she was doing something bad, and she needed to be put down a peg.”

He says, “Really. Well, all I know is you wanted her to stay away from me and now you got what you wanted.”

I tell him, “You sound like you’re mad or something because you’re not going to see her.”

Rashad says, “There you go reading into stuff. I’m just pointing out how crazy it happened that’s all.”

I roll my eyes at him and say, “Okay, if you say so.”

He then goes, “By the way what are you doing?”

I tell him, “If you must know I am researching some stuff about a court case spell. I’m trying to do a spell for good now. Isn’t that what you want me to do?”

He says, “Look I’m sorry that I have been hard on you, but I just want you to focus on our family too not just spells.”

I say, “Yea, I got you”, while walking out the room with my laptop to research in peace. I didn’t need his self- righteousness getting my vibe down. I loved magic and this is who I am, and his nagging was not going to change it.

The next morning, I go find my materials for Nisha’s boyfriend’s court case. According to Jewel, a great way to secure a victory is to read Psalms 35 from the Bible. Her being the Christian Witch, I decide to take her word for it and include it in my spell. But I also use my kitchen witch skills to create an oil for him to use. I go get my herbs and oils and mix them together. While making the oil I recite Psalms 35 and chant “The court case is done, and I have won.”

I go see Nisha and tell her about the oil I made for the court case. I tell her boyfriend how to use it and that he must do his part to ensure that it works.

Dionne, Nisha’s boyfriend, eagerly asks, “Okay, so what I gotta do?”

I tell him, “First you need to go get a Bible and find Psalms 35 and recite it at least three days before the court case. Then I want you to write down the name of your judge and your ex-girlfriend. On the day of the court case, I want you to take the paper and place it in your shoe. This will give you dominance over the judge, so things go in your favor. You also need to wear this oil every day and on the day of the case make sure you rub your whole body down with the oil.”

While telling him what to do, he looks at me like I’m crazy, but he says, “I will try anything. I hope this works.”

Nisha chimes in and says, “Don’t worry it will. My cousin is the best. How do you think I got you to leave your ex?”

He says, “Damn you’re a witch too?”

Nisha says, “Something like that. It’s in our blood.”

Dionne says, “Y'all are crazy” as he walked out of the room.

I tell Nisha, “I gotta go but let me know the outcome. I hope it works out.”

About a week later I hear from Nisha. She says, “Girl all I can say is I appreciate you for your expertise. Dionne cannot stop singing your praises. He did exactly what you told him to do, and the craziest thing happened when we got to court.”

I asked, “What happened?”

Nisha says, “For starters the night before court, his ex-girlfriend calls him and says that she is willing to drop the case if he dumps me. He told her no, then he asked her was I the reason she was going after him and she said yes.”

I say, “That’s crazy that she would admit to that.”

Nisha says, “Yea and then when we get to court, she tells the judge that she no longer wants to petition for full custody and only wants to increase the amount of child support. Of course, the judge gets pissed because she is changing her mind and then after reviewing Dionne’s records the judge sees that his income has not changed so there was no need to increase the child support.”

I say, “Wow.”

Nisha then says, “Wait there’s more. The judge accused her of making frivolous claims. He also blasted her because he said he sees right through her and senses she is jealous and wants to get back at him. She then started crying and the judge dismissed the case and told her next time have proof and not to waste the court’s time.”

I say, "That's how the universe works, and she got exactly what she deserved."

Nisha says, "Yes but I am not going to lie we were shocked but happy. I mean don't get me wrong he doesn't mind paying child support, but his income has not changed, and he gives her more than what the court says but she was just jealous like the judge said."

I say, "I am glad it worked out. If only my life could work out. The other day while I was researching the court case, Rashad came into the room trying to tell me not to do spells and says I am not spending enough time with my family."

Nisha says, "He needs to stop. He is used to you being there 24-7 for him."

I say, "Yea I know. He really is giving off these negative vibes lately. I wish he would see me the same way he sees his little work wife. That whole situation annoyed me and to be honest I don't care if she got into an accident, he better be glad she didn't die. Lord forgive me for speaking death, but she had it coming."

Nisha says, "Ayanna, you must be mad because I never heard you talk like that."

I say, "Yea I was mad at him for not being honest. I know I am not perfect but damn you got this woman calling you her work husband. But I ain't tripping we will work it out even if I got to do a spell on his ass."

Nisha laughed and said, "Yea I know you will. And thank you again and have a good night. Don't kill anybody over there."

CHAPTER 7
KARMA

The next morning while I was in my room getting dressed, I heard Rashad on the phone in the bathroom. I wondered who he was in there talking to. Probably his ole work wife.

After he gets off the phone, he comes in the room looking all suspicious and says, "Good morning, Baby."

I say, "Hmm, Baby? I haven't heard that in a while. You must want something. By the way I heard you talking on the phone before you came in, who were you talking to?"

With a smirk on his face he says, "Well, since you asked it was my work wife."

Without saying a word, I gave him the side eye and said, "Oh now you're calling her your work wife?"

Rashad says, "Ayanna, you know I am just joking with you but that was my boss. Since the accident she's been having a hard time."

I say, "Oh for real."

He says, "Yes, when Janelle was in the accident, the doctors ran some tests on her, and they think they may have found an issue with her heart. They told her she had an irregular heartbeat. She was on the phone damn near in tears telling me about it. You know she doesn't have a lot of friends here so I guess she felt that she could confide in me."

In my most sincere voice I said, "Oh that's too bad. I am truly sorry that happened to her. I wish I could do something to help.

Even though I felt she deserved what she got I had to show some type of sympathy. I didn't want Rashad to think I was some cold-hearted bitch and honestly, I did feel bad because I didn't want anything else to happen to her.

As Rashad sat there, I could sense him wanting to say something else. So, I asked him, "Why do you have that look on your face?"

He then says, "Well I kind of told Janelle that you were into herbs and natural healing. She wanted me to ask you if there is anything that she can take to help with her issues."

I say, "Rashad, are you serious? You want me to help heal the same woman who was making a play for my man?"

Rashad says, "Come on now Ayanna, that's in the past. Not to mention she knows that I am married and you're the only one I have eyes for. Since her accident she keeps it strictly business, no flirty stuff."

"Yea whatever you say. I will see what I can do. But just like I said the other day, my spells are all convenient when you want me to help people but when I do spells for myself it's a problem."

"I know, and I apologized for that. From now on I will let you do you and I will not say anything bad about you doing spells."

Then out of the blue he comes over and kisses me and tells me he loves me. That really made me feel good and I felt like I had my husband back.

While I thought about not helping Janelle, at that moment I knew I had to help her in any way I could. Now don't get me wrong I didn't feel bad for what I did because she deserved it, but I wanted to help her because no one deserves sickness. For some reason I felt like it was my duty.

That weekend I decided to gather all my herbs and make a detox tea for Janelle. In addition to tea, I brought my crystal quartz which was good for healing.

As I walked into Janelle's condo, it was not what I imagined. To my surprise she had plants all over with fresh roses on her living room table and pictures of her loved ones in the corner. I somewhat imagined her as a luxury, bougie type rather than fresh flowers and earthy type girl. I guess you should never judge a book by its cover.

I sat down on the living room chair, and we began to talk. She went on how Rashad just raved about how I was into herbs and liked helping people with all types of issues.

I quickly tell her, "I am not a doctor, but I research a lot about herbs and think most issues can be resolved with natural remedies and even healing crystals. I don't know how you feel about it, but your mental state is sometimes the reason for a lot of physical issues too."

Janelle says, "Well I am game for anything you got. I don't want to be 32 years old with heart problems. The doctors gave me a whole list of heart conditions that I may have. I am just scared at this point."

I say, "I don't want that to happen either. First you need to start drinking this tea, it has herbs to help you get rid of toxins and cleanses your liver. You also need to start drinking alkaline water and cut meat out of your diet. I know it sounds crazy but the food we eat is the cause of a lot of ailments. The best thing for you now is also to get rid of caffeine, which makes your heart work overtime. If you do what I tell you, you will start feeling better in no time."

Janelle said, "I tried going vegan, but I never stuck with it, and I love my morning coffee. It's going to be hard giving up caffeine and meat. But I will do anything to ensure my heart issues go away. What is that in your hand?"

"Oh, this is a crystal. Crystals carry vibrations and they have healing properties. I recommend using this at night under your pillow or even hold it when you meditate or pray. I know it may sound crazy, but you can place the crystal on your heart and visualize being healthy. Keep in mind that positive thoughts manifest positive outcomes so if you think positive the next time you get tested your results will be better."

Janelle says, "Wow. You taught me a lot today. I don't want to sound rude but are you like a witch or something?"

I say, "If you must know, my friends like to call me a Kitchen Witch."

Janelle says, "For real. That's so cool. Do you do spells and stuff?"

I say, "Yes, I do." I laughed, thinking she had no idea I did a spell on her.

Janelle says, "Wow. Well, let me not get on your bad side but for real you don't have a spell to heal me?"

I tell her, "I don't want to make any guarantees, but I can probably do a healing spell on you if you trust me."

She says, "I will try anything at this point."

I tell her to lay down and take out more of my crystals. I place them around her body and place one on her head. I take the healing oil I made and rub her body down in the oil. I tell her to close her eyes and I start to chant the spell, "Angels from above I ask that you make Janelle's body whole and healed. Remove the sickness to show that God's love is real."

I repeat this over and over until Janelle screams. I asked, "Are you okay?"

Janelle says, "It felt like electricity was running through my body. Did you feel it?"

I said, "No but sometimes with energy work you can feel the pain or sickness being removed from your body."

She says, "It felt like something was being removed from me and I saw a bright light. I don't know what you did but I feel different."

I told her, "That's normal. If you want, I can come back in a couple of days, and we can continue to work until your next appointment."

Janelle says, "Okay that would be good. I don't know what you did but it felt good."

Over the next couple of weeks, I performed healing work on Janelle as she continued to drink the detox tea. I was surprised that she was so trusting of me. Then one day out of the blue she tells me that she wants to apologize for making me feel uncomfortable.

I asked her, "What do you mean?"

She says, "Well at the party I called Rashad my work husband. That was not called for. And I will be honest I tried to get him to go out with me. We never kissed or anything like that but I was flirting with him but that was before I met you. To be honest I have been with married men before and Rashad is one of the good ones. He turned me down and I was just asking him to show me around town. I am truly sorry and between you and me, when I was in the accident, I did think I must have done something wrong to deserve this. Must be my karma."

I tell her, "I accept your apology and as my Aunt Nadine used to say, "You make your own karma." So just focus on getting healthy and healed and you can make up for it by being a better person."

Janelle says, "Thank you. You are so kind to me, and I don't deserve it."

As we finished the last healing session, I told Janelle to sit down on the floor and close her eyes. I took out my candles and placed them around her. I recited the healing chant again and as I started to speak; she began to cry.

When she opened her eyes, I asked her if she was okay.

She said yes but she told me that while she was sitting there, she had a vision of her grandmother saying everything would be okay.

I smiled and said, "That is a good sign. Loved ones often come around when you become spiritually connected."

Janelle said, "You are so powerful. Thank you for all that you have done for me. I will let you know when my results come back."

The session with Janelle gave me confidence in my healing abilities. While Janelle came into my life in an awkward way, I am glad we found each other. I got to truly show how powerful I was and help someone in need. This felt good.

While Janelle promised to call me after receiving her results, she ended up calling Rashad first. He comes in the room and says, "Guess what? Janelle texted me and said that her test results came back, and they didn't find any irregularities with her heart. They think the irregular beating could have been caused by her caffeine usage or spike in blood pressure, but they ruled out anything like heart disease. She also said that this was the wakeup call that she needed to get her life on track, and she credits you for helping her see that."

"Wow she said all that?"

"Yep, I knew you could help her. I am so glad to have you as my wife."

I smiled and said, "Thank you!" It felt good to be admired and loved by my husband again.

CHAPTER 8

STAY AWAY SPELL

It was now apparent that with every spell I do I get faster and better results. It feels good to know that I can help others. Especially with serious issues such as Janelle. I was proud to be on my way to becoming a healer just like my Aunt Nadine. As I sat there reflecting on my journey, I was proud that my husband had stopped with his negative comments. Life was good but as I basked in the glory, a phone call interrupted my thoughts.

I answered and said, "Hello?"

"Hey Ayanna. What are you up to?"

It was my cousin, Michael, Aunt Nadine's son. I was glad to hear from him.

I say, "Hey Michael, I'm just relaxing. What are you doing?"

He says, "Nothing just taking a break from working. I decided to call you since I haven't spoken to you in a while."

I say, "Now come on cousin, I know you better than that. You must have something on your mind."

He says, "Well since you asked. I have an issue with this crazy girl I was dating."

I say, "Uh oh. Did you get her pregnant?"

He screams, "Hell No! I barely kissed this girl."

Continuing with the questions, I ask, "Well you must have cheated?"

Michael says, "No! Damn Cuz. You think the worst of me, don't you?"

I tell him, "Not at all. I'm just trying to figure out what would have a girl mad at you that's all. You know we're blood so I am going to ride for you no matter what."

Michael says, "Yea ok. For a minute I thought you were on her side."

I say, "How can I take sides when I don't even know what happened or even know this girl."

He says, "For starters I met her while I was working. She needed a tow and I helped tow her car to the auto parts store. We got to talking and since then we've been dating for a couple of months. I ain't even had sex with her yet and I am damn glad too."

I laugh and say, "Okay so what makes her crazy?"

He says, "When she first came over, she did a drive by. No call, no text, she just drove by my house and then on the second trip around the block she comes knocking on my door. So, you know I didn't like that. Then when she came into my house, she checked the closets and the back yard to see if I had another girl over."

Surprised by her behavior, I asked, "Are you serious? That is crazy. Why are you still dealing with her?"

He says, "Honestly, that was just the beginning. One time she called me when I was working, and I couldn't answer the phone. Since I didn't answer she blows up my phone and calls me back-to-back for the next fifteen minutes. I almost cursed her out. Then just yesterday, I'm towing a car and the lady that I was helping was in the background talking. Of course, she hears the lady and swears that I was cheating with someone. That was the last straw. I told her it would be best if we didn't see each other anymore because I can't deal with that jealousy and obsessive shit."

I asked, "What's the problem since you already let her go?"

Michael says, "That's just it she won't leave me alone. Since I dumped her, she won't stop calling me. She keeps texting; saying she misses me. I even blocked her number, but she found me on social media and sent me messages on there too. I'm telling you Ayanna; I cannot get away from her. She also drives by my job and my house. She never gets out, but I can see her on the security cameras. When I called her out on it, she denied it. She says she was dropping somebody off. I really need this girl out of my life, and I know you're just the person to do it."

I tell him, "Dang Michael that's some crazy stuff. It reminds me of the time when I was being stalked."

Michael says, "Yea I thought about that, and I know my momma helped you so now it's time for you to help me."

I laughed so hard because he was dead serious. I could tell he'd had enough of this girl. Michael never comes to me with his problems, so I know it's something serious.

I tell him, "I know how you feel, so of course I am going to help you out. Let me go see what I can do. I will call you back in a couple of days."

He says, "Don't make me wait that long, this is a life-or-death situation."

I tell him, "It's not that serious but I will call you back. I want to get some guidance from the Ancestors for this situation."

He says, "Well you and the Ancestors do what y'all gotta do. I will be here waiting."

As I got off the phone, I felt bad for Michael. I knew the feeling of having a stalker. Not knowing if someone is watching you and having to look over your back. That feeling was all too familiar. My late Aunt Nadine helped me get rid of my stalker, so I had to help Michael. But that was so many years ago, I could not recall what she did to get rid of him, all I remember was using black candles.

I rumbled through her old books trying to find out what she had put in the spell all those years ago. Unfortunately, I could not find anything. While I knew the internet had tons of spells something told me I needed Aunt Nadine's fail proof formula.

That night I decided to meditate and call upon the spirit of Aunt Nadine. As I sat in the middle of the floor, I lit a white candle and saged myself and the room. Then I said, "I call upon the Ancestors and Aunt Nadine. I ask that you provide me with ways to protect Michael from negative energy." As I spoke those words all I could hear was a loud ringing in my ear. I snapped out of my meditation and crawled into bed. While in bed I said a prayer again to the Ancestors and a special good night to Aunt Nadine. After the prayer I said, "See you in my dreams." I looked over at my husband sound asleep. He didn't mind me speaking with spirits. I thanked God for bringing him into my life because any other man would have called me crazy.

That night I slept peaceful but even though Aunt Nadine was not in my dreams I remember distinctly seeing a red pen and a small black notebook. I sit and think where have I seen that notebook before? Then, it came to me, in my cabinet with Aunt Nadine's things there was a black notebook. For some reason I never opened it. I always thought it was an old phone book with phone numbers. I rumbled through the boxes and find the notebook. And there it was, Aunt Nadine's Stay Away spell written in red ink. I look up to the ceiling and say thank you to the Ancestors. Without them and my dream I would have never found this.

In the book she outlined the herbs needed to get someone especially the law to stay away. While Michael wasn't running from the law, he needed to hide his whereabouts from that crazy ass girl. Me being a kitchen witch all the herbs I needed such as basil and bay leaf were already in my cabinet. I also used olive oil and a black candle but what I did not have was a picture of this girl. To make the spell work I needed this. While it could be done without it, it was more powerful if I had her picture.

I called Michael that morning and he tells me her name. I print out her picture from social media. While this girl looked nice and sweet, she hid her crazy ways from the internet. Based on her social media profiles she seemed to be a well-respected nurse who worked in the pediatric unit of the hospital. How could someone that smart be so crazy.

I went over to Michael's house that night to help him with the spell. I told him all the things I had and what we were going to do. I also told him how my dream brought me to the spell.

Michael tells me, "You definitely have a gift Ayanna, just like my momma."

I say, "Thank you Michael and I even helped Rashad's boss with a healing ritual. You should meet her because she needs some male energy besides my husband."

He says, "Maybe I can meet her after I get this crazy girl out of my life."

I say, "Yea, you're right about that."

He says, "Well let's get on with the spell."

I say, "Dang Michael, don't rush me. This girl must've really scared you."

He shook his head and said, "You know what I ain't even gonna respond to that."

I say, "Okay you know I am just joking Michael. But let's get to it."

I take out my herbs, crystals, and candles. I explain each item and why I have it.

I tell him, "First start with the black candle, for obvious reasons. Black is definitely for your protection of that crazy heffa, and I have rosemary herbs, bay leaf and cayenne pepper. I want you to take all the herbs and place them in a bowl. Then place the crystals around the candle. Now when I light the candle you can repeat after me, "Protect me from negativity, in and out of my home, keep Michelle Hanson away from my home." Now, to make the spell be effective I want you to take her picture and burn it. This symbolizes her being erased out of your life. Then take the ashes and dump them somewhere but not near your home. I also want you to take the herbs and place them in front of your doorstep. This will help keep her away from you. Also, every day until the candle burns out repeat the spell words that I gave you."

Michael, looking at me with relief, said okay to everything I was telling him.

As I left Michael, I had a feeling that his bad days with this crazy girl were over. I lowkey wanted to meet this girl so I could tell her off and to get the hell away from my cousin, but I will let the magic handle it.

The next couple of days I hadn't heard from Michael, so I decided to go over and check on him.

I knocked on the door and he immediately let me in.

I tell him, "I haven't heard from you lately. Are you okay? Have you heard from Michelle?"

He says, "Nope. But guess what?"

I asked, "What? Did something happen?"

He says, "Yea but something good. Ole girl was riding by my house last night and she decided to get out. I saw all this on my security camera. She made it to my front door and just while I was going to open the door to curse her out, she started to walk back to her car. It was as if she just changed her mind."

I say, "Well, we did do protection of your home. That's how you know the spell is working. We blocked negativity from coming in and that just means she was up to no good."

He says, "Yea you're right. Hold up before we jinx ourselves, here she is calling me from a blocked number."

I say, "For real, you got to be kidding me." I looked over at Michael and asked, "What did she say?"

He says, "I don't know I didn't answer. She just texted me though."

I asked, "What does the text say?"

Michael reads the text, "Hey. I am outside your house. Can you come out and talk? I just want to clear the air."

I say, "Is she serious? You got to be kidding, she is a desperate one."

Michael says, "I am not responding to her message."

I tell Michael, "No go ahead and text her back. Tell her you will be outside, and I will go out and take care of it. Plus, you know she ain't setting foot in the house. That's why she wants you to come outside."

Agreeing with me, Michael says, "Yea you're right. It is odd she wants me to come outside. What if she has a gun or something?"

I say, "I don't think she is that crazy to have a gun but just to be on the safe side, go get your gun and I will get my taser. I will go out there first and see if I can talk some sense into her."

Michael says, "Okay let me get my piece. I got your back Cuz."

I walk outside and see her leaning back on the hood of her car.

After I notice that her hands are free of weapons, I introduce myself to her.

I say, "Hello, I am Michael's cousin, Ayanna. What's your name?"

Michelle says, "My name? Don't act like you don't know. I am Michelle. You're probably one of Michael's side chicks."

I shook my head in disbelief of this dumb chick. Then I politely said, "Like I said I am his cousin and Michael wanted to know why are you here? He said he didn't want to see you again."

Michelle says, "I wanted to see him face to face and since I didn't feel comfortable going inside the house, I wanted to have somewhere neutral to talk."

I ask her, "Okay so what do you have to say?"

She says, "Since Michael is acting like a punk ass and won't come see me face to face, you can tell him I am done chasing him."

I say, "Chasing him, well I don't think he ever asked you to chase him. Better yet I think he asked you to leave him alone."

She says, "Girl please. He's the one who asked for my number."

I tell her, "Yea but once he found out how crazy you were he wanted to leave you alone."

She says, "Well whatever, but you can tell Michael with his punk ass that I am done with him."

Out of nowhere I hear Michael yell out, "Who the hell are you calling a punk?" I look around and see Michael running outside to the car. I guess he was watching and listening the whole time. I guess her calling him a punk was getting to him.

Smiling, Michelle says, "See I knew you would come out to see me."

Michael says, "Girl I only came out here to see why you're calling me a punk."

Michelle says, "I don't have to explain myself."

Michael then tells her, "Well how about you get out of my yard before I call the police."

She then says, "Michael all that ain't called for. I just wanted to give you one last chance to change your mind since I had a new guy ask me out."

He says, "I'm good. You can go ahead and keep your date with your new man because I don't want anything to do with you."

As her and Michael were arguing, I started to chant quietly under my breath for her to leave. After about the third repetition, I looked over at them and heard Michelle say, "Michael, I am going to give you your wish and leave."

And just like that she got into her car, put on her shades, and zoomed off down the street in her black Honda with a missing hubcap. Hopefully that would be the last we would see of her.

A surprised Michael asked, "Did you see that? That girl gotta be bipolar."

I say, "Well I don't care what she is as long as she is gone. You see how the protection spell worked because the whole time she stayed near her car, never stepping foot near the house."

He says, "Yea you're right."

I say, "Plus I was over here chanting while y'all were arguing."

He said, "Oh okay well thank you. It seems like she is gone for good."

I say, "Yea, good riddance."

As me and Michael went back in, I was relieved that it worked out.

Seemingly tired, Michael said, "Thanks Ayanna. I knew that whole scenario was all because of you."

I say, "Cousin, its power in the tongue. Earlier today I was hoping to see her in person. And just like that I got my wish. I told you I am a master manifester."

He says, "Yea I believe you. But I can't get over how she was calling me a punk but if I went and pushed her in the car, she would be calling the police on me."

I tell him, "Yep, you got that right. I think deep down that's what she wanted so she could call the cops on you. But she didn't know were heavily protected around here. By the blood and the herbs. Plus, she ain't even got her priorities straight, worried about a man when she needs to be finding that missing hubcap."

We both laugh. Michael says, "Ayanna, you're crazy but you speak the truth, Cuz."

I say, "I know it."

Then as I picked up my purse to leave, I reminded Michael of my Halloween party that I was having.

I tell him, “I want you to come because we haven’t hung out in a while.”

He says, “Yea I will be there, as long as there are no seances. You remember what happened last time with that Ouija board?”

Laughing, I said, “You will never let me live that down.”

“Nope that was a crazy experience. I don’t have time for any ghosts haunting me.”

“It won’t be any of that anymore. I learned my lesson,” I said as I left.

CHAPTER 9

THE FERTILITY RITUAL

As I thought about the conversation that I had with Michael, I remembered that I needed to call everyone and remind them about my party. The first person on the list was my cousin Nina. She was sweet and quiet unlike her sister Nisha. While Nina was like a big sister to me, she had become the family member who you always invite but never shows up. She blamed this on her introverted personality and said that we drain her energy. Being a self-proclaimed introvert, she always stressed that she can only take so much people interaction, even from her own family. Knowing this, I had to call her and stress the importance of the party since I had not seen her in a while.

I called her up and said, “Hey Nina. My long-lost cousin, how are you?”

Laughing Nina said, “Ayanna, you need to stop it. It hasn’t been that long.”

“It sure does feel like it. I didn’t want to disturb you, but I wanted to remind you of my Halloween party that’s coming up. You’re still coming right?”

“I guess so, but I’ve been feeling kind of sorry for myself.”

I asked, “Why? You shouldn’t be feeling like that. Is there anything I can do to help?”

“Actually, you might be able to help me. I’ve been to every doctor in this town, and they all tell me they don’t know why I haven’t gotten pregnant yet. I’ve been trying for the last six months. This doesn’t make any sense.”

“Oh, I am sorry. I had no idea.”

“Yea I know I really haven’t told anyone. I’ve just been feeling sad for myself. But you’re the so-called kitchen witch. What herbs should I be using to get pregnant?”

“Offhand you probably need to get some red raspberry leaf or red clover. Those are good herbs that you can buy as a tea. I can probably make some for you if you want?”

“Yes, I will do anything. Actually, I don’t know why I didn’t think about you first. I know it's some ritual or something you can do for me.”

“Well, I guess but you know I may have to do a reading on you to determine what steps to take next. Sometimes people have blockages, mental or physical that keeps them from getting pregnant.”

“Well, I don’t know what it is. But I know you can help me, right?”

“Yes. I will do all I can. I am going to do some research and then let you know what I think.”

“Okay and Ayanna, I love you. I know we gave you flack when you first started with all the magic and stuff, but you have helped so many, and I can’t wait for you to help me.”

I was glad that my family saw me as the powerful witch that I wanted to become. I have stretched myself and my skills so much this year, but I don’t know if I could do a fertility ritual. This was going to be tough.

Before even thinking about doing a ritual, I had to tap into Nina’s mind. From what I got it appeared that while Nina’s body was ready for a baby her mind was not. I see limiting beliefs that may cause her to think she may not be a good mother. While her mother was good to them, she did lack some motherly qualities. I think this was the missing piece. She needed to clear her mind and remove the negative thoughts of her not being a good mother.

As I thought about what I could do to help her, I knew my fellow witches would be able to help get Nina pregnant. I decided to get the girls together so we could do the ultimate fertility ritual.

When we met up, I told the girls about Nina's fertility issue. We discussed the perfect fertility ritual with each of us bringing our own expertise. For me you know I was going to do my thing with the herbs and oils.

I tell the girls, "We're going to need peppermint oil, lavender, damiana, and lotus flower."

Drea says, "You're definitely a kitchen witch. The only thing you named were herbs."

I laugh and say, "The combination of the herbs and oils are great for fertility. I will also make her a tea with the herbs to get her womb ready for a baby. And Drea since you're so concerned about my herbs, what you got going on over there?"

Drea says, "Honestly, I am thinking of using the Goddess Venus of Love because a baby needs to be conceived in love and then invoke the Goddess Fortuna for good luck. I also want to try my hand at calling on Ostara. She is the goddess of new beginnings and fertility."

I then say to Jewel, "Okay, now it's your turn what you got for us, Christian Witch?"

She says, "I have been researching, and I think I want to use a fertility chant, but I was thinking about using a Bible verse that talks about fertility. Those words are powerful and can bring forth a new life."

I say, "Great, so we are all set. Let's get everything together by Sunday so we can do the ritual. Sundays are about new beginnings, and we can use the Sun's powerful energy also. This ritual is going to be one for the books. I am so excited."

When Sunday came, we all gathered at Nina's house. Her husband was gone so it was just us. I don't know what her husband would have said if he would have known we were doing a ritual. Nina's husband was cool, but he always got scared when anyone brought up magic. He was one of those southern boys who swore his mama or daddy had roots put on them because of their bad luck. So, I know he didn't want anything to do with herbs or magic let alone a ritual.

I walked into Nina's house with the girls right behind me. As I greeted Nina, I asked her where Jaylin, her husband was.

She said, "He went out of town to see his brother. Plus, I didn't want him all up in my business, you know how he feels about roots."

I say, "Yea, scared as hell," as we all laughed.

Jewel says, "If he knew we were going to help him have a baby he wouldn't be scared."

Nina says, "Yea but I am ready. What do I need to do?"

I tell her, "First we want you to sit in the chair and relax your mind. When I first did my reading, it seemed like your mindset was off. I want you to envision being the best mother, no conflicting thoughts. It is necessary when manifesting to have clear and concise thoughts. Only think of being a mother, no what ifs or doubting yourself."

She said, "Ok."

I then lit some sage to cleanse out negative energy. With the sage burning, I brought out the candles and placed them in a circle. I instructed her to get inside the circle and rub the oil on her stomach, head, feet, and heart. While Nina laid there, Drea called upon the Goddesses Venus, Fortuna, and Ostara.

Drea said, "Oh goddesses, I ask that you come before me and bring new life into Nina. Bring the new life by love, positivity, and great fullness." As she spoke these words, we held hands leaving Nina to rub her stomach.

Jewel, then recited her chant: "In my stomach a baby will grow, with the power of God let it be so." We repeated this over and over until we felt the energy flowing into Nina. After the chant, Jewel recited the bible verse, "As it says in Deuteronomy 7:14, you will be blessed more than any other people; none of your men or women will be childless, nor will any of your livestock be without young."

As she spoke the bible verse, I could see the words as if they were coming out of her mouth with so much energy.

Jewel then said, "Everyone let's form a circle and push the remaining energy into Nina." While Nina rubbed her stomach, we chanted and chanted, until our energy was depleted.

As we closed the ritual, I told Nina to drink the tea and rub the oil on her stomach every day while reciting the bible verse.

Drea told her, "You may also call upon the Goddesses when you make love to your husband. This will help to get the love energy going for him and you and put you in the mind frame to make a baby."

As I looked over at Nina, I saw that she was crying.

I asked, "Nina, what's wrong?"

Wiping her tears, she said, "Nothing. I am just so thankful for y'all helping me. I know I used to be skeptical of what you do but I am grateful for you. I know this is going to work, I can just feel it in my soul."

I say, "Aww, you are welcome. That's what we do, we didn't study with Miss Jay for nothing."

Jewel says, "Yea she is right. We love to help others especially when you have exhausted all other options. Everything is going to be okay. You will be pregnant in no time."

As we said our good-byes and walked to our cars I said to the girls, "I just want to thank you all for helping my cousin, but I also want to tell you about a vision I had while chanting."

Drea asked, "What did you see?"

I told her and Jewel, “I saw all three of us working together.”

Drea asked, “What do you mean working?”

I explained, “I mean just like we did in there but at our own place. That leads me to my next thought of us starting a business together. Like a store.”

Jewel asked, “Are you serious?”

I said, “Yea. Wouldn’t that be cool? I already got a name for it, The Power of Three.”

Drea said, “I see somebody has been watching *Charmed*.”

We laughed. But I say, “I am serious y'all.”

Jewel said, “You know that’s not a bad idea. Let’s do some research then we can put a plan together.”

As I made my way home that night, I was hyped up on the possibility of opening a store. As I came home, I was pleasantly surprised by my husband.

As soon as I walked in the door, Rashad said, “Hey Baby, I am glad to see you.”

Sarcastically, I said, “Really, that’s a change.”

He then says, “How can you say that? You know I am always glad to see you.”

I tell him, “You must want something.”

He says, “Yea, some of your good loving.”

I laughed, and said, “I knew it had to be something.”

While I joked, I am glad I had my loving and carefree husband back. It felt like my life was getting back on track. Not to mention I was too high on life thinking about opening an actual store where I could share my gifts to the world.

CHAPTER 10

NEW BEGINNINGS

When I woke up the next morning, I was greeted with breakfast in bed from my husband. He really was getting back to his loving and sweet personality.

I asked him, "So what's up with the nice and loving husband act?"

He says, "Baby, I just want you to be happy."

I tell him, "I am, and I am glad we are back to us being happy and no arguments. It makes my life even better. I am also excited about some other stuff I got going on too. I can't tell you yet but it's going to be big."

He says, "Alright then, keep your secrets," as he walked off.

While I knew this store idea was going to work out, I didn't want to say anything yet.

As I got dressed that morning, I was already looking at locations for the store. The next couple of weeks, I had the girls buy in and they were entrusting me to be the head of this project.

As the weeks went on, I found a great building with the perfect location for our store. I met up with the girls so we could meet the realtor and see the store front.

We all walked into the building, as the realtor gave us a play by play of the building.

The realtor said, "This unit has a lot of space where you can have products, and your register would be over there and then they have the back where you could store inventory as well. What kind of store are you ladies going to have?"

I tell her, "It's going to be called The Three Witches and it will be a store with all types of magical products, like tarot cards, herbs and crystals."

The realtor says, "Oh wow. That's interesting. I don't think we have anything like that around here."

I tell her, "Yea we know."

As we looked around, I took it upon myself to envision what the store would be like. I tell them, "We could put our crystals here in the front and then books over by the window. Oh, then we can have tarot readings in the back. I don't know about y'all, but I think this is the perfect spot."

Drea says, "Ayanna, you are too hype. But you're right, I like this location and I can see your vision. I'm in."

I asked, "What about you, Jewel?"

Jewel says, "I knew this was the spot when we first came in, I was just waiting to see what y'all thought."

Drea says, "Yea right."

I asked, "So are we all in agreement, we want to sign the lease?"

Jewel and Drea both say, "Yes."

We then tell the realtor that we are ready to sign the lease. She said she would send the documents over later that day.

On the ride home, I told the girls about my husband finally acting right.

Drea says, "It's about time."

I say, "I know right."

Jewel asks, "What about the party you're having?"

I say, "Oh I almost forgot about it since I been so busy with the store stuff, but the party is still on, Halloween night."

As the weeks went on, I was loving getting things together for our new store. I couldn't wait to tell my family. As we gathered on Halloween night, I was ready to party and tell everyone the big news.

Before the party, I went into my room and lit a candle. Since Halloween is all about the dead, I lit a candle for the dead ancestors who came before me. As I lit the candle, I sat in silence and called out my ancestors' name. I could feel the air get cold and heard a whistling noise in my ear. I didn't know who or what was there, but something was different about the energy.

I called out, "If anyone is here, make yourself known." I didn't hear anything, but it felt as if someone was standing right behind me. A little scared, I stood still and heard a voice say, "Girl, you know you can do anything you put your mind to." I opened my eyes and there in front of me stood my grandfather. I called out, "Grandpa is that you?"

He said, "Yea who do you think it is? You called for your ancestors didn't you."

I stood in awe, too surprised to say anything. He said, "Girl you look like you done seen a ghost," as he laughed.

I let out a sigh and said, "Grandpa is that really you?"

He said, "Didn't I tell you it was me. I don't have a lot of time; I just want to say I am proud of you and remember to keep your faith in God and everything will be okay." Then he tipped his hat and disappeared in thin air.

I laid down on the bed with my hands over my eyes. Was that really my grandfather's ghost? While I was in shock, I was happy that he came to talk to me and represented all the ancestors who came before me. They were proud of me; I just knew I was on the right path with what I was doing. While he said to have faith in God, I knew some people thought just because I am a self-proclaimed witch, I don't believe in God, but I do. God is the ultimate creator and I love and respect him. I have just chosen to serve him in a different way. That's what I call living in my own truth and forging my own path.

While I laid there, I heard a knock on the door. I called out, "Yea, who is it?"

"It's me Amir." I opened the door and told Amir to come in. He then asked me, "Mommy what are you doing?"

I say, "Nothing, just resting before the party."

He says, "Well its almost time for the party, people are at the door."

Before going to the door, I got my witch hat since I was none other than a witch for Halloween. I went to the door and greeted my first guests. It was Nina and her husband. As they walked in, they seemed happier than usual. I couldn't put my finger on it, but something was different. Nina had not shared anything with me since the fertility ritual, so I wasn't sure if it had worked or not.

Minutes later the other guests came in, which included my cousin Michael and my husbands' boss, Janelle. I must admit that I have come a long way since trying to put a hex on her. She's actually a sweet girl when she is not trying to seduce my husband. I can't say that were friends but since she didn't have lots of friends, I decided to invite her.

As she came in, I could see that Michael had already cornered her and was occupying her time. If I were a man, I would occupy her too since she was wearing a naughty nurse costume. At least I knew she wouldn't be coming for my man tonight.

My cousin Nisha, wearing an Angel costume, asked, "Who is the naughty nurse?"

I said, "Oh that's Rashad's boss that I told you about."

Nisha says, "What, you let her come into your home?"

I say, "Yes, since I let her know that Rashad was happily married, I haven't had any problems out of her. I figured her and Michael would hit it off since he dumped that crazy girl he was dealing with."

Nisha says, "Oh yea, seems like they are feeling each other. You over there making love connections and stuff, but you need to be helping me get a new man. Don't you see Dionne is not here with me. After all I did to help him, he ended up going back to his baby momma."

I say, "Girl, I can't help you. You're beyond help. I don't have a spell strong enough for you."

She goes, "Ha, ha, very funny."

As the night went on, we played games, danced, and had fun. Then as the night ended, I decided that I would make a toast.

I stood in the middle of the room, with my glass, holding it high trying to get everyone's attention. "Alright, everyone, I have a toast to make." Everyone then stood up as I had their attention.

I said, "I just want to thank everyone for coming and let you all know I love you. I also want to call up Jewel and Drea."

As they made their way next to me, I could see everyone's faces trying to figure out what was going on. As the girls stood by my side, I said, "We want you all to be the first to know that we have decided to open a store. It's going to be called "The Three Witches."

Everyone clapped and smiled. I was on cloud nine. Leave it to Nisha to yell out, "Congrats cousin. What are you going to be selling?"

I say, "Of course it's a metaphysical store so we will be selling crystals, books, candles and all that jazz."

Nisha says, "Oh wow, I am excited. I am going to be your first customer. Actually, can I work for you?"

I say, "Girl you are crazy. We will see once we get started up."

Then suddenly, Nina yelled out and waved her hand and said, "Hold up y'all, since everyone is giving announcements, I have one of my own."

We all stood in silence waiting to see what she was going to say. Nina is the quietest, so I knew it had to be something serious.

As she stood up, she pulled up her shirt and showed off her small baby bump, and said we are going to have a new addition to the family. We all cheered and smiled. This was wonderful.

Then Nina said, “I just want to say thank you to the three witches, they are responsible for this pregnancy. Their fertility ritual removed the blockages and helped me to conceive. I am forever grateful to you ladies.”

Everyone smiled and some of us were crying. This was such a joyous occasion. A new baby and a new business, that I helped to create.

This was the ultimate high to know that you have helped someone bring another life into the world. And to think once our business is open, we will have many more opportunities to help others.

CHAPTER 11

SHUT UP SPELL

For the next few weeks I was busy getting our store ready. We had already ordered inventory and we were getting fixtures together for the store. I decided to visit the store to drop off some of the inventory. As I unpacked the inventory; I got a strange text on my phone from an unknown number. I opened the text and it read, "I know what you did."

Who could this be texting me? And what do they think I did?

Thinking it was a scam or spam message, I ignored the text. Then a call comes in from an unknown number. For some reason my heart was beating fast, I didn't know who was on the other line. I decided to let the call go to voicemail.

Then I see that the unknown person left a voicemail message. I decided to listen to the message and while I listened I immediately figured out exactly who it was. It was no other than, Lashika, Jayvon's wife. My life was going good and now she wanted to come into my life and ruin everything. I listened to the message again:

"Hey Ayanna. This is Lashika, Jayvon's wife. I saw the texts you sent him and not to mention the pictures. You always did want my man but guess what you can't have him. Better yet I think I should tell your husband how you out here being a hoe with my husband since you want to ruin my marriage. And the next time I call you better answer unless you want your secret out."

My worst nightmare was rearing its ugly head. I never thought that my secret would come out about me and Jayvon. What was I going to do? Should I just confess and tell Rashad? Or ignore it? I wasn't scared of Jayvon's wife, but I was afraid that she would tell my husband. I didn't know what to do about this situation.

Later at home, still in shock, I wondered how did Jayvon's wife find out about us? I wondered if he told her, or did she go through his phone? Better yet why did Jayvon keep those texts and pictures of us in his phone? He should've deleted all that stuff. Unsure of what to do I go over my cousin's Nina's house and talk it out with her. She always has the best advice.

I pulled up to Nina's house and when I got out, I looked around to make sure no one was following me. As I walked in Nina says, "Hey Ayanna. Why were you looking around like that? Do you think that Lashika girl is following you or something?"

I sighed, "Nina I don't know? This girl has turned my world upside down with one phone call. I was high on life at the store earlier and now I am afraid that my husband may find out about my; well, I don't know what to call it. It wasn't an affair because it was just a kiss. I don't know what it was."

Nina said, "Let's just call it an entanglement."

I laughed and said, "Girl I guess that's what it was."

As I sat down on the sofa, my stomach felt queasy. Nina went and got me some water and told me to chill out.

I said, "Okay I'm calm now. What do you think I should do?"

Nina said, "I think you should ignore her. Do you really think that she will tell Rashad? Think about it, she would need his phone number or address. I don't think she has all that information about you or Rashad."

I say, "You know what you're right. She probably only got my number by snooping in Jayvon's phone. I'm tripping for no reason."

Nina then said, "Even though she is probably making empty threats, if it continues you probably need to confront her about it."

Unsure, I said, "I don't know Nina. I just want the whole thing to go away. Maybe if I don't respond she will go away."

Nina said, "It can go either way. I say don't reply yet, just wait. If she sends another message or calls you, talk to her and you can tell whether she is bluffing or for real."

I say, "You're right. That's what I am going to do."

Nina also says, "And if she continues to threaten you, remember you're the witch. Hex her ass and your ex for putting you in this position."

I laughed and did not expect that from my sweet cousin. But she was right, I am a witch, and I don't mind putting her in her place with the help of magic.

As days went by, I had not heard from Lashika. Then one morning, as I stepped out of the shower, I see that I had a missed call. She didn't leave a voicemail this time, instead she sent a text message saying, "Don't think I forgot about you."

That was it, I decided to text her back and say, "You need to leave me the hell alone."

That must have gotten her mad because she immediately called my phone. Tired of being scared, I answer and say, "What the hell do you want?"

She says, "Oh don't be rude to me you are the one who messed with my husband."

I say, "I didn't mess with your husband he was the one coming on to me."

Lashika then says, "That's not what the text you sent said. You were telling him how good he looked and not to mention pictures of you all together."

I will admit I never should have let him take pictures of us on the phone as I regret it, but she was taking it the wrong way. I tried to level with her.

"Look Lashika. I'm going to keep it real I did meet up with Jayvon, but nothing happened. It was only two times. He also made it seem like you were cool with it."

"Hmm Really. I think you're lying."

"Did you even ask Jayvon what happened?"

"Yes, I did, and he denied the whole thing, so I know something happened. That's why I am going to tell your husband. Everyone thinks you're so perfect and can't do any wrong. I'm going to let all your dirty laundry out."

"Look I am not going to sit here and let you accuse me of something I didn't do. You better leave my husband out of this."

"Nope. You brought my husband in it, so I am doing the same. Just wait till I get his phone number and your address, it's on." She then hung up.

What was I going to do? This bitch would not stop. While I decided to visit the store to take my mind off things, I see Jewel had beat me to it.

When I walk in, Jewel looks at me and asks, "What's going on with you, something seems off?"

I tell Jewel, "You always could read people well. To be honest I have a girl trying to ruin my life."

She asks, "Ruin your life? What girl?"

I say, "Jayvon's crazy wife, Lashika. His wife somehow found out about us, and she is threatening to expose me to my husband."

Jewel says, "Damn that's crazy. Your situation sounds like a Lifetime movie but why are you stressing over this shit when you're a witch. You better get in your kitchen and cook up a spell."

I say, "I don't know, I feel like I don't have any energy left for spell casting right now. I just want to confess to Rashad and get it over with."

Jewel says, "Hell no, I'm not going to let you put your marriage at risk for some jealous unhappy housewife. Leave it to me I am going to help you with a Shut-Up Spell."

Reluctant to agree with Jewel, I say, "I don't know about that."

Jewel says, “You don’t know! Ayanna, now is not the time to be scared. Like Miss Jay said, she didn’t raise no scared witches. And like they say, if your ass scared, go to church! If not, meet me at my house after we’re finished here. I got something that’s going to shut her ass up.”

After realizing Jewel was right, I left the store and made my way to her house. I sat in the car, waiting for her to pull up. Since we left at the same time, I wondered how I made it before she did. She then pulls up and says, “Sorry I made you wait I had to make a stop.”

We walk into Jewel’s house, and she says, “I had to pull out the big guns for this.”

While talking, she pulls out an animal’s tongue. Shocked to see what she pulled out, I ask, “Is that a real tongue?”

She says, “Yep, this is a cow’s tongue. The tongue represents Lashika’s tongue and we’re gonna tie it up and bind it to shut it up.”

I was disgusted by the tongue, but I had to do what I had to do to shut her up.

Jewel instructed me to rub the herbs all on the tongue. It felt rough but firm, but all the blood seemed to be dried out. I had to close my eyes and turn my head away from smelling it. After that she handed me some yarn as I tied the tongue up. I must admit this made me feel like a boss ass witch since I had only seen this type of thing in movies.

As I tied up the tongue, Jewel completed the spell. The nasty part was over, and we stood there reciting the words from Psalms 31: “Let their lying lips be silenced, for with pride and contempt they speak arrogantly against the righteous.” She told me to wait for action in three days and that should shut her up.

After 48 hours, I got a strange call from Jayvon. What did he want?

I answered and he told me that he found out his wife was harassing me. I asked him, “Why did you leave those pictures in your phone? And the text messages?”

He replied, "I know that was careless and I am sorry she is calling you. I told her to stop, and I deleted all the pictures and messages from my phone. I checked her phone too and removed any proof of you and me being together."

I tell him, "That's the least you could do since you're the reason I am even in this mess."

He says, "I know, I am sorry she gets that way. I had to calm her down because the last time she did this the girl brought harassment charges against her."

I say, "Oh so she's done this before?"

He says, "Yea so I am trying to stop her before it gets to that point."

I tell Jayvon, "Well you better stop her if not she got something coming for her."

I didn't tell him, but I had already done something to shut that ass up.

The next day I get a call from Lashika. Surprisingly when she comes on the phone her tone has changed. She starts with, "Ayanna, I just want to clear the air with you. I am not upset with you; I am mad at my husband. To be honest I talked with my therapist, and she told me you're not the one I should be mad at."

I am stunned. I stand there with the phone to my ear, thinking she is bi-polar or wondering what changed her mind. But I know what did it, that shut up spell. Not to mention she is probably scared of getting charges against her again.

She goes on to say, "I just want to move on. Let me and my husband have our relationship and you do the same."

Maybe I was putting fuel on the fire, but I said, "Okay, but you are crazy if you think I want your cheating ass husband."

She says, "Ayanna, I'm trying to be nice. I am gonna let that slide just don't meet my husband anymore and I will let you and your husband be happy. Bye."

After hanging up I was sure this girl was bipolar and needed her meds. I hope that is the last time she bothers me.

The next day I woke up to several texts and missed calls from Lashika, vowing to harm me if I ever mess with her husband again. I decided to call her and put this situation to rest. As I call her phone, Jayvon answers.

He says, "Ayanna, why are you calling my wife's phone?"

I say, "She's the one who's been harassing me, she called and texted me about ten times last night."

Jayvon says, "Oh well I am sorry about that, but she is in the hospital now."

I ask, "Hospital? Why?"

He says, "She was walking down the stairs in the basement this morning and she slipped and fell. She has a head injury and her jaw is broken. She had to get her mouth wired so I am answering her calls since she can't talk."

Surprised I say, "Oh damn, I am glad she is okay."

He says, "Yea right. Did you have anything to do with this? You are the witch."

I say, "How dare you blame me for an accident."

He says, "I am sorry, I am just frustrated. But you won't be hearing from Lashika anytime soon because of her head injury she will be heavily medicated and will not have time for any harassment."

I say, "Well I hope she gets better. I hope you have a nice life Jayvon because this will be the last time that you talk to me." Since I didn't want to hear anything more from him, I immediately hung up the phone after that. I wanted nothing more to do with him or his crazy ass wife.

I couldn't wait to tell Jewel what happened. That damn spell shut her up alright.

Lashika had me nervous, but that fear is gone now. That's one last thing I have to worry about. Now I can focus on my new store.

As I go to Jewel's house to talk about Lashika's accident Jewel says, "I told you I had to pull out the big guns. That will teach her to make threats on you. Now you can relax and get ready for our store."

Later that night I sat in the bed thinking how lucky I was to have such a great friend like Jewel who has my back no matter what. I was also grateful to have a loving husband who was faithful to me unlike Jayvon. I know I'm not perfect but it's great to have family and friends that support me no matter what.

Something then came over me and I had the sudden urge to pray. I put my hands together and thanked God for his blessings. However, in true kitchen witch form, after my prayer I lit a candle to honor the ancestors while being surrounded by crystals. I must admit being a kitchen witch is not for the weak, but I am glad to be the one to walk this magical path.

Bonus Chapter

Poetry from the Kitchen Witch

Yep, I am a WITCH!!!

Woman in charge of her life and reaching her goals

Independent and smart with beauty and soul

Tell you what she wants,

Call the shots and deserves the best

Has mastered the art of letting go of the stress

Down on My Knees

I burned my candles all day and all night
I will do anything to make it all right
Between me and you
I even resorted to doing voodoo
At the same time, I'm here praying down on my knees
Begging and pleading for you to come back to me
I need you in my life
I am ready to be your wife
The mother of your child
You know this begging ain't even my style
But I'm going to get you back because you're my twin flame
And to be honest I know I'm to blame
I dare you to look into my eyes
and allow me to apologize
For all the lies that I told
I know you still love me deep down in your heart and soul
You know it's real love and not lust
I know you need time to think about us
In the meantime, I will set you free
But in my heart, I know you will come back to me.

Glowing and Growing

They say you're glowing
I say you're growing
Into the woman you want to be
Letting go of all the pain and misery
that happened in the past
Like they say in church, trouble don't last
always
That's right, like Tupac said
Keep your head up
Even though you're fed up
Now is the time
For you to shine
Get up and go make it better
It's time to get your life together
Stop stressing and get your blessings
Say your prayers and if you want go cast a spell
But you better dispel
those lies they tell
And let go of all the stress
So, your dreams will come true and manifest
into the physical right before your eyes,
Then watch all the haters fall to their demise.

Zodiac Loves

I had a Capricorn man, and he was the GOAT
Like Aaliyah said, he knew how to rock the boat
Even though I loved him, we would always fuss and fight
But end up making love by the end of the night
He would kiss me, touch me then say put it on my face
After we were done, he'd tell me how good I taste
Even though he was the best
He would never let me get rest
Waking me up in the middle of the night to do it again
What we used to do had to be a sin
But my Scorpio man was hot like fire
He was every woman's desire
Chocolate brown skin and a nice gentle touch
Why did I love this man so much?
But now I remember, he had the best kiss
That's definitely what I miss
And how he would rub me and kiss me down to my feet
Not to mention he knew how to put me to sleep
But after I left him, I got with a Gemini
Like Johnny Gill, he made me say MY, MY, MY
He would always tell me to get on top and ride
All those nights of making love outside

In the park, after dark
This man really turned me into a freak
When I see him, my knees used to get weak
I can't believe I'm like Mary J. Blige, reminiscing on the love we had
Like Usher, I got it bad
But I had to let all of them go
Now I have the King of the Jungle, a roaring Lion Leo
Who is loyal to a fault and vows to never let me go.

Mistress

He called me his mistress, but I felt more like a side piece

All those nights when I would call his phone

I would wish and hope that he was alone

He would only call me when his wife was gone

But I would pick up and say baby I miss you so much

I yearn and wish for your touch

He would then reply

I love you, that I can't deny

I can't wait to see you on the weekend

so, we can really get it in

Dinner, movie and then a room at my favorite hotel

But remember to keep it a secret and don't ever tell

I promise to keep it on the down low

Only me and you will know

But it's killing me because I need a man to give me all his time

I want someone to be all mines

I know we got a connection but I'm tired of using protection

I want the love that's real and raw and someone I can give my heart to

I'm sad to say that it is not you

But like Erykah Badu,

I will see you

In the next lifetime, maybe then you will be mine.

Go For It

Take me for my flaws and all

I make mistakes but I get up when I fall

I tell myself you must do better

Because in my heart I am a go getter

Yes, sometimes I had to break the rules

To show them that my momma didn't raise no fool

And in the end the naysayers became my footstool

Because they don't know the power of the mind

If you look inside, all the answers you will find

This will help you to open your eyes and see

That you are worthy of having a life of love, peace, and prosperity.

I Affirm

I affirm I am whole, healed, and free
I am making a promise to myself to focus on me
I affirm to protect my peace at all costs
I am not Rick Ross
but my mantra for life is “I am the boss.”
I affirm to be a woman who knows her worth
Because without us there would be no earth
I affirm to let my light shine
And be the woman God made me to be
Embracing all my divine feminine energy
I affirm that I will have all that I desire
Keep going for my dreams even if I get tired
From this day forward, I affirm, declare and decree
I am the Woman who I want to be.

HEX MY EX

I put a hex on my ex because he promised to give me the world
When I confessed my love, he went back to his ex-girl
But I'm the type of chick that don't sing no sad song
I like to get even and make him feel bad for doing me wrong,
Then take him for all that he's worth
Deep down inside I want to bury him down under the earth
Since I can't do that, I will go cast a spell
By lighting his picture on fire and damn him to hell,
Then take a piece of his hair
Call forth his downfall and blow it into the air
And hope that he has a life of misery and despair
So don't be surprised when he is somewhere laying in a ditch
That's what he gets for messing with a witch and a bitch.

Manifest

I just want the fortune, forget the fame
I don't need everyone to know my name
I manifest the life that I want with grace and ease
I am the only one who I need to please
Creating and shifting my reality
A master manifester, yea that's me
I see what I want and claim it as mine
Your new reality starts in your mind
Write down your thoughts and speak them into the air
That's how you manifest, with the help of the universe,
Now sit back and let your thoughts do the rest
Get focused and clear on how you want your life to be
If you have the will, you will see
Your vision come true right before your eyes
Like Maya Angelou, you will rise
So, meditate and pray; Let God and the ancestors show you the way
You will see your vision come true clear as day
But remember this is your life; you have the final say.

Spell

He put a spell on me without saying a word
There were no nouns, there were no verbs
Maybe it was his hands or even his eyes
I loved the way he slowly touched my thighs
Or maybe it was the way he would use his tongue
As he kissed my neck under the sun,
And the times that he would pull my hair and make me scream
Only the freaks know what I mean
Not to mention those nights when he used whip cream
Now I'm thinking it was a spell
The way he used to make love to me so well
I never had a man to love me so right
Making love under the moonlight
Feenin' all because we had a fight
Baby if you can hear my plea
Please come back to me
I want to feel the things that you do so well
Please put me under your spell.

Let Me Be Free

Let me be free to wear my hair in coils, kinks, or even a ‘fro
Showing my individuality not the status quo
Let me be free to dig my toes in the sand
I have melanin in my skin, so I don’t wear suntan
Let me be free to create my own identity
And not be judged for expressing my sexuality
Whether I love a woman or man,
Let me be free to hold their hand
I am free when I pray to God, Allah or even Mother Earth
And sometimes I will even thank the Universe
I like to be free to dance and move my body to the beat
Always daring and never falling to defeat
Let me be free to drive my car in peace
And not be in danger of the police
Let me be free to choose what I want for my life
I can be a mother, CEO, or even a Housewife
I will not let society put limits on what I can do
I honor my ancestors because of all they went through
Without them there would be no me
Because of them I am free
And able to live a life that they could never see.

www.ingramcontent.com/pod-product-compliance
Lightning Source LLC
LaVergne TN
LVHW050601160826
845677LV00011B/2404